Bylow Hill

George Washington Cable

Contents

BYLOW HILL

BY

George Washington Cable

"Father," laughed the daughter, "isn't this rather youngish?"

I
RUTH AND GODFREY

The old street, keeping its New England Sabbath afternoon so decently under its majestic elms, was as goodly an example of its sort as the late seventies of the century just gone could show. It lay along a north-and-south ridge, between a number of aged and unsmiling cottages, fronting on cinder sidewalks, and alternating irregularly with about as many larger homesteads that sat back in their well-shaded gardens with kindlier dignity and not so grim a self-assertion. Behind, on the west, these gardens dropped swiftly out of sight to a hidden brook, from the farther shore of which rose the great wooded hill whose shelter from the bitter northwest had invited the old Puritan founders to choose the spot for their farming village of one street, with a Byington and a Winslow for their first town officers. In front, eastward, the land declined gently for a half mile or so, covered, by modern prosperity, with a small, stanch town, and bordered by a pretty river winding among meadows of hay and grain. At the northern end, instead of this gentle decline, was a precipitous cliff side, close to whose brow a wooden bench, that ran half-way round a vast sidewalk tree, commanded a view of the valley embracing nearly three-quarters of the compass.

In civilian's dress, and with only his sea-bronzed face and the polished air of a pivot gun to tell that he was of the navy, Lieutenant Godfrey Winslow was slowly crossing the rural way with Ruth Byington at his side. He had the look of, say, twenty-eight, and she was some four years his junior. From her father's front gate they were passing toward the large grove garden of the young man's own home, on the side next the hill and the sunset. On the front porch, where the two had just left him, sat the war-crippled father of the girl, taking pride in the placidity of the face she once or twice turned to him in profile, and in the buoyancy of her movements and pose.

His fond, unspoken thought went after her, that she was hiding some care again,--her old, sweet trick, and her mother's before her.

He looked on to Godfrey. "There's endurance," he thought again. "You ought to have taken him long ago, my good girl, if you want him at all." And here his reflections faded into the unworded belief that she would have done so but for his, her own father's, being in the way.

The pair stopped and turned half about to enjoy the green-arched vista of the street, and Godfrey said, in a tone that left his companion no room to overlook its personal intent, "How often, in my long absences, I see this spot!"

"You wouldn't dare confess you didn't," was her blithe reply.

"Oh yes, I should. I've tried not to see it, many a time."

"Why, Godfrey Winslow!" she laughed. "That was very wrong!"

"It was very useless," said the wanderer, "for there was always the same one girl in the midst of the picture; and that's the sort a man can never shut out, you know. I don't try to shut it out any more, Ruth."

The girl spoke more softly. "I wish I could know where Leonard is," she mused aloud.

"Did you hear me, Ruth? I say I don't try any more, now."

"Well, that's right! I wonder where that brother of mine is?"

The baffled lover had to call up his patience. "Well, that's right, too," he laughed; "and I wonder where that brother of mine is? I wonder if they're together?"

They moved on, but at the stately entrance of the Winslow garden they paused again. The girl gave her companion a look of distress, and the young man's brow darkened. "Say it," he said. "I see what it is."

"You speak of Arthur"--she began.

"Well?"

"What did you make out of his sermon this morning?"

"Why, Ruth, I--What did you make out of it?"

"I made out that the poor boy is very, very unhappy."

"Did you? Well, he is; and in a certain way I'm to blame for it."

The girl's smile was tender. "Was there ever anything the matter with Arthur, and you didn't think you were in some way to blame for it?"

"Oh, now, don't confuse me with Leonard. Anyhow, I'm to blame this time! Has Isabel told you anything, Ruth?"

"Yes, Isabel has told me!"

"Told you they are engaged?"

"Told me they are engaged!"

"Well," said the young man, "Arthur told me last night; and I took an elder brother's liberty to tell him he had played Leonard a vile trick."

"Godfrey!"

"That would make a much happier nature than Arthur's unhappy, wouldn't it?"

Ruth was too much pained to reply, but she turned and called cheerily, "Father, do you know where Leonard is?"

The father gathered his voice and answered huskily, laying one hand upon his chest, and with the other gesturing up by the Winslow elm to the grove behind it.

She nodded. "Yes!... With Arthur, you say?... Yes!... Thank you!... Yes!" She passed with Godfrey through the wide gate.

"That's like Leonard," said the lover. "He'll tell Arthur he hasn't done a thing he hadn't a perfect right to do."

"And Arthur has not, Godfrey. He has only been less chivalrous than we should have liked him to be. If he had been first in the field, and Leonard had come in and carried her off, you would have counted it a perfect mercy all round."

"Ho-oh! it would have been! Leonard would have made her happy. Arthur never can, and she can never make him so. But what he has done is not all: look how he did it! Leonard was his beloved and best friend"--

"Except his brother Godfrey"--

"Except no one, Ruth, unless it's you. I'm neither persuasive nor kind, nor often with him. Proud of him I was, and never prouder than when I knew him to be furiously in love with her, while yet, for pure, sweet friendship's sake, he kept standing off, standing off."

"I wish you might have seen it, Godfrey. It was so beautiful--and so pitiful!"

"It was manly,--gentlemanly; and that was enough. Then all at once he's taken aback! All control of himself gone, all self-suppression, all conscience"--

"The conscience has returned," said the girl.

"Oh, not to guide him! Only to goad him! Fifty consciences can't honorably undo the mischief now!"

"Did I not write you that there was already, then, a coolness between her and Leonard?"

"Yes; but the whole bigness and littleness of Arthur's small, bad deed lies in the fact that, though he knew that coolness was but a momentary tiff, with Isabel in the wrong, he took advantage of it to push his suit in between and spoil as sweet a match as two hearts were ever making."

"It was more than a tiff, Godfrey; it"--

"Not a bit more! not--a--bit!"

"Yes!--yes--it was a problem! a problem how to harmonize two fine natures keyed utterly unlike. Leonard saw that. That is why he moved so slowly."

"Hmm!" The lover stared away grimly. "I know something about slowness. I suppose it's a virtue--sometimes."

"I think so," said the girl, caressing a flower.

"Ah, well!" responded the other. "She has chosen a nature now that--Oh me!... Ruth, I shall speak to her mother! I am the only one who can. I'll see Mrs. Morris some time this evening, and lay the whole thing out to her as we four see it who have known one another almost from the one cradle."

Ruth smiled sadly. "You will fail. I think the matter will have to go on as it is going. And if it does, you must remember, Godfrey, we do not really know but they may work out the happiest union. At any rate, we must help them to try."

"If they insist on trying, yes; and that will be the best for Leonard."

"The very best. One thing we do know, Godfrey: Arthur will always be a passionate lover, and dear Isabel is as honest and loyal as the day is long."

"The day is not long; this one is not--to me. It's most lamentably short, and tomorrow I must be gone again. I have something to say to you, Ruth, that"--

The maiden gave him a look of sweet protest, which suddenly grew remote as she murmured, "Isabel and her mother are coming out of their front door."

II
ISABEL

There were two dwellings in the Winslow garden,--one as far across at the right of the Byington house as the other was at the left. The one on the right may have contained six or eight bedchambers; the other had but three. The larger stood withdrawn from the public way, a well-preserved and very attractive example of colonial architecture, refined to the point of delicacy in the grace and harmony of its details. Here dwelt Arthur Winslow, barely six weeks a clergyman, alone but for two or three domestics and the rare visits of Godfrey, his only living relation. The other and older house, in the garden's southern front corner, was a gray gambrel-roofed cottage, with its threshold at the edge of the sidewalk; and it was from this cottage that Isabel and her mother stepped, gratefully answering the affectionate wave of Ruth's hand,--Mrs. Morris with the dignity of her forty-odd years, and Isabel with a sudden eager fondness. The next moment the two couples were hidden from each other by the umbrageous garden and by the tall white fence, in which was repeated the architectural grace of the larger house.

Mother and daughter conversed quietly, but very busily, as they came along this enclosure; but presently they dropped their subject to bow cordially across to the father of Ruth, and when he endeavored to say something to them Mrs. Morris moved toward him. Isabel took a step or two more in the direction of the Winslow elm and its inviting bench, but then she also turned. She was of a moderate feminine stature and perfect outline, her step elastic, her mien self-contained, and her face so young that a certain mature tone in her mellow voice was often the cause of Ruth's fond laughter. As winsome, too, she was, as she was beautiful, and "as pink as a rose," said the old-time soldier to himself, as he came down his short front walk, throwing half his glances forward to her, quite unaware that he was equally the object of her admiration.

Though white-haired and somewhat bent he was still slender and handsome, a most worthy figure against the background of the red brick house, whose weathered walls contrasted happily with the blossoming shrubs about their base, and with the green of lawn and trees.

"Good-afternoon, Isabel. I was saying to your mother, I hope such days as this are some offset for the Southern weather and scenery you have had to give up."

"You shouldn't tempt our Southern boastfulness, General," Isabel replied, with an air of meek chiding. She had a pretty way of skirmishing with men which always brought an apologetic laugh from her mother, but which the General had discovered she never used in a company of less than three.

"Oh! ho, ho!" laughed Mrs. Morris, who was just short, plump, and pretty enough to laugh to advantage. "Why, General,"--she sobered abruptly, and she was just pretty and plump and short enough to do this well, also,--"my recovered health is offset enough for me."

"For *us*, my dear," said the daughter. "My mother's restored health is offset enough for us, General. Indeed, for me"--addressing the distant view--"there is no call for off-set; any landscape or climate is perfect that has such friends in it as--as this one has."

"Oh! ho, ho!" laughed the mother again. Nobody ever told the Morrises they had a delicious Southern accent, and their words are given here exactly as they thought they spoke them.

"My dear," persisted Isabel, rebukingly, "I mean such friends as Ruth Byington."

Mrs. Morris let go her little Southern laugh once more. "Don't you believe her, General--don't you believe her. She means you every bit as much as she means Ruth. She means everybody on Bylow Hill."

"I'm at the mercy of my interpreter," said Isabel. "But I thought"--her eyes went out upon the skyline again--"I thought that men--that men--I thought that men--My dear, you've made me forget what I thought!"

They laughed, all three. Isabel, with a playful sigh, clutched her mother's hand,

and the pair drew off and moved away to the bench.

"He puts you in good spirits," said the mother, breaking a silence.

"Good spirits! He puts me in pure heartache. Oh, why did you tell him?"

"Tell him? My child! I have not told him!"

"Oh, mother, do you not see you've told him point-blank that it's all settled?"

"No, dearie, no! I only see that your distress is making you fanciful. But why should he not be told, Isabel?"

"I'm not ready! Oh, I'm not ready! It may suit him well enough to hear it, for he knows Leonard is too fine and great for me; but I'm not ready to tell him."

"My darling, he knows you are good enough for any Leonard he can bring."

"Oh yes, on the plane of the Ten Commandments." The girl smiled unhappily.

"But precious, he loves Arthur deeply, and thinks the world of him."

"Mother, what is it like, to love deeply?"

The query was ignored. "And the old gentleman is fond of you, sweetheart."

"Oh, he likes me. What a tame old invalid that word 'fond' has grown to be! You can be fond of two or three persons at once, nowadays. My soul! I wish I were fond of Arthur Winslow in the old mad way the word meant when it was young!"

"Pshaw, dearie! you'll be fond enough of him, once you're his. He's brilliant, upright, loving and lovable. You see, and say, he is so, and I know your fondness will grow with every day and every experience, happy or bitter."

"Yes.... Yes, I could not endure not to give my love bountifully wherever it rightly belongs. But oh, I wish I had it ready to-day,--a fondness to match his!"

"Now, Isabel! Why, pet, thousands of happy and loving wives will tell you"--

"Oh, I know what they will tell me."

"They'll not tell you they get along without love, dearie. But ten years from now, my daughter, not how fond you were when you first joined hands, but what you have"--

"Oh yes,--been to each other, done for each other, borne from each other, will be the true measure. Oh, of course it will; but there's so much in the right start!"

"Beyond doubt! Understand me, precious: if you have the least ground to fear"--

"Mother! mother! No! no! What! afraid I may love some one else? Never! never! Oh, without boasting, and knowing what I am as well as Leonard Byington knows"--

"Oh, pshaw! Leonard Byington!"

"He knows me, mother,--as if he lived at a higher window that looked down into my back yard." The speaker smiled.

"Then he knows," exclaimed the mother, "you're true gold!"

"Yes, but a light coin."

"My pet! He knows you're the tenderest, gentlest dear he ever saw."

"But neither brave nor strong."

"Oh, you not brave! you not strong! You're the lovingest, truest"--

"Only inclined to be a bit too hungry after sympathy, dear."

"You never bid for it, love, never."

"Well, no matter; I shall never love any one but myself too much. I think I shall some day love Arthur as I wish I could love him now. I never did really love Leonard,--I couldn't; I haven't the stature. That was my trouble, dearie: I hadn't the stature. I never shall have; and if it's he you are thinking of, you are wasting your dear, sweet care. But he's going to be our best and nearest friend, mother,--he and Ruth and Godfrey, together and alike. We've so agreed, Arthur and I. Oh, I'm not going to come in here and turn the sweet old nickname of this happy spot into a sneer."

"Then why are you not happy, precious?"

"Happy? Why, my dear, I am happy!"

"With touches of heartache?"

"Oh, with big wrenches of heartache! Why not? Were you never so?"

"I'm so right now, dearie. For after all is said"--

"And thought that can't be said"--murmured Isabel.

"Yes," replied the mother, "after all is said and thought, I should rather give you to Arthur than to any other man I know. Leonard will have a shining career, but it will be in politics."

"I tried to dissuade him," broke in the daughter, "till I was ashamed."

"In politics," continued Mrs. Morris,--"and Northern politics, Isabel. Arthur's will be in the church!"

"Yes," said the other, but her whole attention was within the fence at their side, where a rough stile, made in boyhood days by the two brothers and Leonard, led over into the garden. She sprang up. "Let's go, mother; he's coming!"

"Who, my child?"

"Both! Come, dear, come quickly! Oh, I don't know why we ever came out at all!"

"My dear, it was you proposed it, lest some one should come in!"

The daughter had moved some steps down the road, but now turned again; for Ruth and Godfrey, returning, came out through the garden's high gateway. However, they were giving all their smiles to the greetings which the General sent them from his piazza.

"Come over, mother!" called Isabel, in a stifled voice. "Cross to the hill path!" But before they could reach it Arthur and Leonard came into full view on the stile. Isabel motioned her mother despairingly toward them, wheeled once more, and with a gay call for Ruth's notice hurried to meet her in the middle of the way.

III
ARTHUR AND LEONARD

Godfrey passed over to the General, who had walked down to his gate on his way to the great elm. Out from behind the elm came the other two men, Arthur leading and talking briskly:--

"The sooner the better, Leonard. Now while my work is new and taking shape--Ah! here's Mrs. Morris."

Both men were handsome. Arthur, not much older than Ruth, was of medium height, slender, restless, dark, and eager of glance and speech. Leonard was nearer the age of Godfrey; fairer than Arthur, of a quieter eye, tall, broad-shouldered, powerful, lithe, and almost tamely placid. Mrs. Morris met them with animation.

"Have our churchwarden and our rector been having another of their long talks?"

The joint reply was cut short by Godfrey's imperative hail: "Leonard!"

As Byington turned that way, Arthur said quietly to Mrs. Morris, "He's promised to retain charge"--and nodded toward Isabel. The nod meant Isabel's financial investments.

"And mine?" murmured the well-pleased lady.

"Both."

The two gave heed again to Godfrey, who was loudly asking Leonard, "Why didn't you tell us the news?"

"Oh," drawled Leonard smilingly, "I knew father would."

"I haven't talked with Godfrey since he came," said Mrs. Morris; and as she left Arthur she asked his brother: "What news? Has the governor truly made him"--

"District attorney, yes," said Godfrey. "Ruth, I think you might have told me."

"Godfrey, I think you might have asked me," laughed the girl, drawing Isabel toward Arthur and Leonard, in order to leave Mrs. Morris to Godfrey.

Arthur moved to meet them, but Ruth engaged him with a question, and Isabel turned to Leonard, offering her felicitations with a sweetness that gave Arthur tearing pangs to overhear.

"But when people speak to us of your high office," he could hear her saying, "we will speak to them of your high fitness for it. And still, Leonard, you must let us offer you our congratulations, for it is a high office."

"Thank you," replied Leonard: "let me save the congratulations for the day I lay the office down. Do you, then, really think it high and honorable?"

"Ah," she rejoined, in a tone of reproach and defense that tortured Arthur, "you know I honor the pursuit of the law."

Leonard showed a glimmer of drollery. "Pursuit of the law, yes," he said; "but the pursuit of the lawbreaker"--

"Even that," replied Isabel, "has its frowning honors."

"But I'm much afraid it seems to you," he said, "a sort of blindman's buff played with a club. It often looks so to the pursued, they say."

Isabel gave her chin a little lift, and raised her tone for those behind her: "We shall try not to be among the pursued, Ruth and Arthur and I."

The young lawyer's smile broadened. "My mind is relieved," he said.

"Relieved!" exclaimed Isabel, with a rosy toss. "Ruth, dear, here is your brother in distress lest Arthur or we should embarrass him in his new office by breaking the laws! Mr. Byington, you should not confess such anxieties, even if you are justified in them!"

His response came with meditative slowness and with playful eyes: "Whenever I am justified in having such anxieties, they shall go unconfessed."

"That relieves *my* fears," laughed Isabel, and caught a quick hint of trouble on Arthur's brow, though he too managed to laugh. Whereupon, half sighing, half singing, she twined an arm in one of Ruth's, swung round her, waved to the General as he took a seat on the elm-tree bench, and so, passing to Arthur, changed partners.

"Let us go in," whispered Leonard to his sister, with a sudden pained look, and instantly resumed his genial air.

But the uneasy Arthur saw his moving lips and both changes of countenance. He saw also the look which Ruth threw toward Mrs. Morris, where that lady and Godfrey moved slowly in conversation,--he ever so sedate, she ever so sprightly. And he saw Isabel glance as anxiously in the same direction. But then her eyes came to his, and under her voice, though with a brow all sunshine, she said, "Don't look so perplexed."

"Perplexed!" he gasped. "Isabel, you're giving me anguish!"

She gleamed an injured amazement, but promptly threw it off, and when she turned to see if Leonard or Ruth had observed it they were moving to meet Godfrey. Mrs. Morris was joining the General under the elm.

"How have I given you pain, dear heart?" asked Isabel, as she and Arthur took two or three slow steps apart from the rest, so turning her face that they should see its tender kindness.

"Ah! don't ask me, my beloved!" he warily exclaimed. "It is all gone! Oh, the heavenly wonder to hear you, Isabel Morris, you--give me loving names! You might have answered me so differently; but your voice, your eyes, work miracles of healing, and I am whole again."

Isabel gave again the laugh whose blithe, final sigh was always its most winning note. Then, with tremendous gravity, she said, "You are very indiscreet, dear, to let me know my power."

His face clouded an instant, as if the thought startled him with its truth and value. But when she added, with yet deeper seriousness of brow, "That's no way to tame a shrew, my love," he laughed aloud, and peace came again with Isabel's smile.

Then--because a woman must always insist on seeing the wrong side of the goods--she murmured, "Tell me, Arthur, what disturbed you."

"Words, Isabel, mere words of yours, which I see now were meant in purest play. You told Leonard"--

"Leonard! What did I tell Leonard, dear?"

"You told him not to confess certain anxieties, even if they were justified."

"Oh, Arthur!"

"I see my folly, dearest. But Isabel, he ought not to have answered that the more they were justified, the more they should go unconfessed!"

"Oh, Arthur! the merest, idlest prattle! What meaning could you"--

"None, Isabel, none! Only, my good angel, I so ill deserve you that with every breath I draw I have a desperate fright of losing you, and a hideous resentment against whoever could so much as think to rob me of you."

"Why, dear heart, don't you know that couldn't be done?"

"Oh, I know it, you being what you are, even though I am only what I am. But, Isabel, you know he loves you. No human soul is strong enough to blow out the flame of the love you kindle, Isabel Morris, as one would blow out his bedroom candle and go to sleep at the stroke of a clock."

"Arthur, I believe Leonard--and I do not say it in his praise--I believe Leonard can do that!"

"No, not so, not so! Leonard is strong, but the fire of a strong man's love, however smothered, burns on without mercy, my beautiful, and you cannot go in and out of that burning house as though it were not on fire."

"And shall Leonard, then, not be our nearest and best friend, as we had planned?"

"He shall, Isabel. Ah yes; not one smallest part of your sweet friendship will I take from him, nor of his from you. For, Isabel, though he were as weak as I"--

"As weak as *I*, you should say, dear. You are not weak, Arthur, are you?"

"Weak as the bending grass, Isabel, under this load of love. But though he, I say, were as weak as I, you--ah, you!--are as wise as you are bewitching; and if I should speak to you from my most craven fear, I could find but one word of warning."

"Oh, you dear, blind flatterer! And what word would that be?"

"That you are most bewitching when you are wisest."

As Isabel softly laughed she cast a dreaming glance behind, and noticed that she and Arthur were quite hidden in the flowery undergrowth of the hill path. They kissed.

"Beloved," said her worshipper, with a clouded smile, as he let her down from her tiptoes, "do you know you took that as though you were thinking of something else?"

"Did I? Oh, I didn't mean to."

Such a reply only darkened the cloud. "Of whom were you thinking, Isabel?"

She blushed. "I was think--thinking--why, I was--I--I was think--thinking"--

she went redder and redder as he went pale--"thinking of everybody on Bylow Hill. Why--why, dear heart, don't you see? When you"--

"Oh, enough, enough, my angel! I take the question back!"

"You *made* me think of everybody, Arthur, you were so sudden. Just suppose I had done so to you!" They both thought that worthy of a good laugh. "Next time, dear," added Isabel,--"no, no, no, but--next time, you mustn't be so sudden. There's no need, you know,"--she blushed again,--"and I promise you I'll give my whole mind to it! Get me some of that hawthorn bloom yonder, and let's go back."

IV
AND BRING DOWN THE REMAINDER

This "hill path" was a narrowed continuance of the street, that led gradually down along the hill's steep face to reach the town and the river meadows. Godfrey, halting before Ruth and her brother, watched the blooming hawthorn, over there, bend and shake and straighten and bend again, above Arthur's unseen hands. Then, glancing furtively back toward Mrs. Morris, he muttered to Ruth, while Leonard gravely looked out across the landscape, "I live and learn."

"So we learn to live," was Ruth's playful reply. To her it was painfully clear that Mrs. Morris, very sweetly no doubt, had eluded Godfrey's endeavors to inform her of anything not to his brother's unqualified praise. In the Bylow Hill group, Ruth had a way of smiling abstractedly, which was very dear to Godfrey even when it meant he had best say no more; and this smile had just said this to him when Isabel and Arthur came into view again. As the two and the three drifted toward each other, Ruth let Leonard outstep her, and joined Godfrey with a light in her face that quickened his pulse.

After a word or two of slight import she said, as they slowly walked, "Godfrey."

"Yes," eagerly responded the lover.

"Down in the garden, awhile ago--did I--promise something?"

"You most certainly did!" She had promised that if he would let a certain subject drop she would bring it up again, herself, before he must take his leave.

"And must you go very soon, now?" she asked.

"I've only a few minutes left," said the lover, with a lover's license.

"Well, I'm ready to speak. Of course, Godfrey, I know my heart."

The young man smiled ruefully. "I've known mine till I'm dead tired of the acquaintance."

Other words passed, her eyes on the ground as they loitered, and after a pause she murmured:--"But I've known my heart as long as you've known yours."

"You've known--What do you--Oh, Ruth, look at me!"

She looked, very tenderly, although she said, "You forget we are observed."

"Oh, observed! Do you mean hope--for me--after all?"

"I mean that if you will only wait until we can get a clear light on this matter of Isabel's--which will most likely be by the next time you come"--

"Oh, Ruth, Ruth, my own Ruth at last!"

"Please don't speak so. I'm not engaging myself to you now."

"Oh yes, you are! Yes, you are! Yes--you--are!"

"No--no--no--listen! Listen to me, Godfrey. I think that now, among us all, we shall manage Isabel's affair well enough, and that the very next time--you--come"--She began absently to pick her steps.

"What--what then?"

"Then you may ask me."

The response of the overjoyed lover was but one or two passionate words, and her sufficient reply, as they halted among their fellows, was to look across the valley with her meditative smile. Isabel took note, but kindly gave a long sigh of admiration, and with an exalted sweep of the hand drew the gaze of the five to the beauties of the scene below. The day was near its end. The long shadow of the great cliff behind Bylow Hill hung over the roofs of the town and over the hither meadows. The sun's rays were laying their last touches upon the winding river, and upon the grainfields that extended from its farther shore. In the upper blue rested a few peaceful clouds, changing from silver to pink, from pink to pearly gray, and on the skyline crouched in a purpling haze the round-backed mountains of another county.

To Mrs. Morris and the General the sight, from the old elm-tree seat, was even fairer than to the youthful group whose forms stood out against the sky, the floral colors of the girls' draperies heightened by the western light. For a while the two sitters gave the perfect scene the tribute of a perfect silence, and then the General asked, as he cautiously straightened his impaired frame, "Has not Isabel been making some--eh--news for herself--and us?"

The lady's lips parted for their peculiar laugh of embarrassment, but the questioner's smile was so serious that she forced her sweetest gravity. "Why, General, according to our Southern ways," she said,--every word mellowed by her Southern way of saying it,--"that's for Isabel to tell you."

"Then why does she not do it, Mrs. Morris?" asked the veteran, who had been district attorney himself once upon a time, and was clever with witnesses.

"Why, really, General, Isabel hasn't had a cha--Oh! ho, ho! I oughtn't to have said that!" Mrs. Morris had a killing dimple, but never used it.

"I suppose--of course"--said the General, "she will say it's--eh--Arthur?"

"Now you're making me tell," she laughed, "and I mustn't! General, Godfrey seems to be going."

In fact, Godfrey was shaking hands with Ruth and Leonard. Now he took the hands of Arthur and Isabel together, and Mrs. Morris laughed more sweetly and with more oh's and ho's than ever; for Isabel sedately kissed Arthur's brother.

Ruth made signs to her father, who answered them in kind. "What does she say, Mrs. Morris? Can you hear?"

"She says they're singing 'your hymn' down in a church under the hill."

"Ah yes." He beamed and nodded to Ruth; but when Mrs. Morris once more laughed, his brow clouded a trifle. "Your daughter, Mrs. Morris"--

The lady broke in with a note of bright surprise, rose, and took an unconscious step forward. The five young friends were advancing in a compact cluster, with measured pace. Ruth and Isabel, in front abreast, and making happy show of the hawthorn sprays, were just enough apart to conceal, except for their superior height, the three lovers, and in lowered tones, but with kindling eyes, the five, incited by Ruth, were singing the song they had caught up from the valley,--the old man's favorite from the days of his own song-time. The General got himself hurriedly to his feet; the shade passed from his brow. The group came close; he stepped out, and Isabel, meeting him, laid her two hands in his, while the halting cluster ceased their song suspensively on a line that pledged loves and friendships too ethereal to clash.

"Isabel,"--he turned up a broadened palm,--"here's my amen to that line;

where's yours?"

With blushing alacrity she laid her hand on his.

"Arthur!" he called, and the lively lover added his to the two. "Now, Ruth!"

"Father!" laughed the daughter, "isn't this rather youngish?" But she laid her hand promptly upon Arthur's, and the lines of the General's face deepened playfully, and Mrs. Morris's dimple did the same, as Godfrey thrust his hand in upon Ruth's, unasked. The matron laughed very tenderly on the key of O while she added her hand, and received Leonard's heavy palm above it. Then Arthur clapped a second hand upon Leonard's, and Leonard was about to lay a second quietly upon Arthur's, when Isabel, rose-red from brow to throat, gayly broke the heap and embraced Ruth.

"Well, honey-girlie," said Mrs. Morris, as she and Isabel reentered their cottage, "wasn't it sweet of them all, that 'laying on of hands,' as Arthur called it?"

"Yes," replied the Southern girl, starting up the cramped old New England stairway to her room. "It was child's play, but it was very sweet of them, and especially of the General."

The mother detained her fondly. "And still, my child, you're not satisfied?"

"Ah, mother, are you blind, stone blind, or do you only hope I am?"

"My dearie!"

"Why, mother, excepting Leonard, we haven't had one word of true consent from one of them."

"Oh, now, Isabel! They'll all be glad enough by and by."

"Yes," said the daughter, from the landing above, "I've no doubt of that."

She passed into her room, closed the door, and standing in the middle of the floor, with her temples in her palms, said, "O merciful God! Oh, Leonard Byington, if only that second hand of yours had hung back!"

V
SKY AND POOL

Arthur and Isabel were married in their own little church of All Angels, at the far end of the old street. "I cal'late," said a rustic member of his vestry, "th' never was as pretty a weddin' so simple, nor as simple a weddin' so pretty!"

Because he said it to Leonard Byington he ended with a manly laugh, for by the anxious glance of his spectacled daughter he knew he had slipped somewhere in his English. But when he heard Leonard and Ruth, in greeting the bride's mother, jointly repeat the sentiment as their own, he was, for a moment, nearly as happy as Mrs. Morris.

"Such a pity Godfrey had to be away!" said Mrs. Morris. It was the only pity she chose to emphasize.

Godfrey was on distant seas. The north-bound mid-afternoon express bore away the bridal pair for a week's absence.

"Too short," said a friend or so whom Leonard fell in with as he came from the railway station, and Leonard admitted that Arthur was badly in need of rest.

At sunset Ruth came out of her gate and stood to welcome her brother's tardy return. Both brightly smiled; neither spoke.

When he gave her a letter with a foreign stamp her face lighted gratefully, but still without words she put it under her belt. Then they joined hands, and he asked, "Where's father?"

"Inside on the lounge," she replied. Her lips fell into their faraway smile, to which she added this time a murmur as of reverie, and Leonard said almost as musingly, "Come, take a short turn."

Indeed it was clear that to go away would be unfair.

They moved on to the Winslow gate, and entered the garden by a path which brought them to a point midway between the old cottage and the larger house. There it crossed under an arch transecting an arbor that extended from a side door of the one dwelling to a like one of the other, and the brother and sister had just passed this embowered spot and were stepping down a winding descent by which the path sought the old mill-pond, when behind them they observed two women pass athwart their track by way of the arbor, and Ruth smiled and murmured again. The crossing pair were Mrs. Morris and Sarah Stebbens, the Winslows' life-long housekeeper, deeply immersed in arranging for Isabel to become lady of the larger house, while her mother, with a single young maidservant, was to remain mistress of the cottage.

The deep pond to whose edge Leonard and Ruth presently came was a narrow piece of clear water held in between Bylow Hill and the loftier cliff beyond by an old stone dam long unused. Rude ledges of sombre rock underlay its depths and lined and shelved its sides. Broad beeches and dark hemlocks overhung it. At every turn it mirrored back the slanting forms of the white and the yellow birch, or slept under green mantles of lily pads. It bore a haunted air even in the floweriest days of the year, when every bird of the wood thrilled it with his songs, and it gave to the entire region the gravest as well as richest note among all its harmonies. Down the whole way to it some one long gone had gardened with so wise a hand that later negligence had only made the wild loveliness of this inmost refuge more affluent and impassioned.

At one point, where the hemlocks hung farthest and lowest over the pool, and the foot sank deep in a velvet of green mosses, a solid ledge of dark rock shelved inward from the top of the bank and down through the flood to a depth cavernous and black. Here, brought from time to time by the Byington and Winslow playmates, lay a number of mossy stones rounded by primeval floods, some large enough for seats, some small; and here, where Ruth had last sat with Godfrey, she now came with her brother.

The habitual fewness of Leonard's words was a thing she prized beyond count. It made Mrs. Morris nervous, drained her mind's treasury, and sent her conversational powers borrowing and begging; Isabel it awed; Arthur it tantalized; to Godfrey it was an appetizing drollery; but to Ruth it was dearer and clearer than all spoken eloquence.

The same trait in her, only less marked, was as satisfying to him, and from one rare utterance to another their thoughts moved like consorted ships from light to light along a home coast. A motion, a glance, a gleam, a shade, told its tale, as across leagues of silence a shred of smoke may tell one dweller in the wilderness the way or want of another. Such converse may have been a mere phase of the New Englander's passion for economy, or only the survival of a primitive spiritual commerce which most of us have lost through the easier use of speech and print; but the sister took calm delight in it, and it bound the two to each other as though it were itself a sort of goodness or greatness.

"They have it of their mother," the old General sometimes said to himself.

There were moments, too, when their intercourse was still more subtle, and now they sat without exchange of glance or gesture, silent as chess players, looking up the narrow water into a sunset exquisite in the delicacy of its silvery plumes, fleeces pink and dusk, and illimitable distances of palest green seen through fan-rays of white light shot down from one dark, unthreatening cloud.

"Leonard," at length said the sister, as if she had studied every possibility on the board before touching the chosen piece, "couldn't you go away for a time?"

And with deliberate readiness the other gentle voice replied, "I don't think I'd better."

While they spoke their gaze rested on the changing beauties of pool and sky, and after the brief inquiry and response it still remained, though the inner glow of their mutual love and worship deepened and warmed as did the colors of the heavens and of the glassing waters. The brother knew full well Ruth's poignant sense of his distresses; and to her his mute tongue and unbent head were a sister's convincement that he would endure them in a manner wholly faithful to every one of the loved hands that had lain under his the evening Godfrey had said good-by.

Indeed, it was clear that to go away--unless he honestly felt too weak to remain--would be unfair to almost every person, every interest, concerned; and such a step was but second choice in Ruth's mind, conditioned solely on any unreadiness he might have uprightly to bear the burden brought upon him by--well, after all, by his own too confident miscalculations in the game of hearts.

To him such flight signified the indeterminate continuance of his sister's maiden singleness and a like prolongation of her lover's galling suspense. To Ruth it stood not only for the loss of her brother, but for the narrowing of their father's already narrowed life,--a narrowing which might come to mean a shortening as well; and it meant also the leaving of Isabel and Arthur to their mistake and to their unskilfulness slowly and patiently to work out its cure. To go away were, for him, to consent to be the one unbroken string on a noble but difficult instrument. These thoughts and many more like them passed to and fro, out through the abstracted eyes of the one, across to the fading clouds, and back through the abstracted eyes and into the responding heart of the other.

At length the sister rose. "I must go to father," she said.

The brother stood up. Their eyes exchanged a gentle gaze and tenderly contracted.

"I will come presently," he replied, and was turning toward the water, when he paused, threw a hand toward the steep wood across the pool, and silently bade her listen.

The note he had remotely heard was rare on Bylow Hill since the town had come in below, and one of the errands which oftenest brought the hill's dwellers to this nook in solitary pairs was to hearken for that voice of unearthly rapture,--a rapture above all melancholy and beyond all mirth,--the call of the hermit thrush.

Now the waiting seemed in vain. The brother's hand sank, the sister turned, and soon he saw her pass from view among the boughs as she wound up the rambling path toward the three homes.

At the top she halted, still longing to hear at his side that marvellous woodnote, and was just starting on once more, when from the same quarter as before it came again, with new and fervent clearness. With noiseless foot she sprang back down the bendings of the path, having no other thought but to find her brother standing as she had left him, a rapt hearer of the heavenly strain.

She reached the spot, but found no hearkening or standing form. The young man's stalwart frame lay prone on the green bank, where he had thrown himself the moment she had left his sight, and his face was buried in the deep moss.

The stir of her swift coming reached his ear barely in time for him, as she choked down a cry that had all but escaped her, to turn upon his back, meet her glance, and drive the agony from his face with a languorous smile. The melting song pervaded the air, but neither of them lifted a noting finger.

Leonard rose to his feet. Ruth gave him a hand and then its fellow, and as he pressed them together she said, "I wish you *would* go away for a time."

He dropped one of her hands, and keeping the other, started slowly homeward; and it was not until they had climbed half the ascent that, with his most remote yet boyish smile, he replied, "I don't think I'd better."

VI
IN THE PUBLIC EYE

August, September, October, November,--so passed the year in gorgeous recession over Bylow Hill. Among their dismantled trees the three homes stood unveiled to the town on the meadows and to travellers who looked from train windows while crossing the river bridge. To those who inquired whose they were there was always some one more than ready to give names and details, and to tell how perfect a bond ever had been--how beautiful a fellowship was yet, now--up there.

Sevenfold they called it, although one of the seven was away; namely, Lieutenant Godfrey Winslow, of the navy, famed for his splendid behavior in the late so-and-so affair. That stately house at the right, they said, was his home what brief times the sea was not.

There lived, it would be added, his younger brother, so rapidly coming into note,--the eccentric but gifted rector of All Angels; whose great success in the heart of a Congregational community was due hardly more to his high talents than to the combined winsomeness and practical sympathies of his beautiful bride, or to the resourceful wisdom and zeal of his churchwarden, Leonard Byington.

"Any relation to Byington, your new political leader in these parts?"

"Same man," the answer would be, and there the narrator was sure to fall into a glowing tribute to the ideal companionship existing between the rector, his bride, the young district attorney, and Ruth Byington.

What made this intimacy the more interesting was, in the eyes of a growing number of observers, that, as they said, "Arthur Winslow was not always an affable man, and was much more rarely a happy one."

Behind and above this popular verdict was that of the old street behind and above the town,--a sort of revised version, a higher criticism. If the young rector, this old street explained, oftener looked anxious than complacent, so in their time, most likely, did St. Paul and St. Peter. If he was not always affable, why, neither are volcanoes; the man was all molten metal within. Anyhow, he filled his church to the doors.

Coaching parties of the vastly rich made the town their Sunday stopping place purely to hear him; not so much because the boldness of his speculations kept his bishop frightened as because he always fused those speculations on, white-hot, to the daily issues of private and public life, in a way to make pampered ladies hold their breath, and men of the world their brows. Such a man, to whom the least sin seemed black and bottomless, yet who appeared to know by experience the soul's every throe in the foulest crimes, was not going to show his joys on the surface in quips and smiles.

"You should have heard," said the old street, "his sermon to husbands and wives! His own bride turned pale. He turned pale himself."

It was wonder enough that even the bride could be happy, at such an altitude, so to speak; immersing herself utterly, as she did, in the interests that devoured him. All Angels forgot his gloom in the radiance of her charms,--the sweet genuineness of her formal pieties, the tender glow and universality of her sympathies, the witchery of her ever ready, never too ready playfulness. It was captivating to see how instantly and entirely she had fitted herself into a partnership so exacting; though it was pitiful to note, on second glance, how the tint and contour of her cheek were losing their perfection, and her eyes were showing those rapid alternations of languor and vivacity which story-tellers call a "hunted look." Yet, oh, yes, she was happy; the pair were happy. It was as a pair that they were happiest. Else, said the old street, they could not keep up the old Winslow-Byington alliance so beautifully.

To the truth of this general outline the three homes' domestics, dominated by Sarah Stebbens, certified with cordial and loyal brevity. Yet when Ruth wrote Godfrey how well things were going, there lurked between her bright lines one or two irrepressible meanings that locked his jaws till they creaked.

In fact, both his brother and hers were "ailing." Both carried a jaded, almost a broken look, and Arthur was taking things to make him eat and sleep; while Leonard had daily accepted more and more of the young rector's complicating cares, until he was really the parish's chief burden-bearer.

"No," he said to his father, "Arthur carries his whole work manfully on his own shoulders."

"But, my son," replied the old General, "don't you see you're carrying Arthur?"

"No, I sha'n't do that," dryly responded the son; but Ruth saw a change on his brow as on that of a guide who fears he has missed the path.

The four young friends spent many delightful evenings together in the Winslow house, with Mrs. Morris and the General on one side at cribbage. Ruth had frequent happy laughs, observing Isabel's gift for making Leonard talk. It gave her a new joy in both of them to have the lovely hostess draw him out, out, out, on every matter in the wide arena to which he so vitally belonged; eliciting a flow of speech so animated that only afterward did one notice how dumb as any tree on Bylow Hill he had been in regard to himself.

"They are bow and violin," said Arthur to Ruth, with his dark, unsmiling face so free from resentment that she gratefully wondered at him, and was presently ashamed to find herself asking her own mind if he was growing too subtle for her.

On these occasions Isabel was wont to court Ruth's counsel concerning her wifely part in Arthur's work, thus often getting Leonard's as well. Sometimes she impeached his masculine view of things, in her old skirmishing way. Then she would turn rose-color once more and mirthfully sigh, while Ruth laughed and wished for Godfrey, and Mrs. Morris breathed soft ho-ho's from the cribbage board.

So came the Thanksgiving season, with strong, black ice on the mill pond, where the four skated hand in hand. Then the piling snows stopped the skating with a white Christmas, the old year sank to rest, the new rose up, and Bylow Hill, under its bare elms and with the pine-crested ridge at its back, sat in the cold sunshine like a white sea bird with its head in its down. And when the nights were frigid and clear its ruddy lights of lamp and hearth seemed to answer the downward gaze of the stars in silent gratitude for conditions of happiness strangely perfect for this imperfect world, and the town marvelled at the young rector's grasp of his subject when his text was, "The heart knoweth his own bitterness."

VII
THE HOUR STRIKES

But on a day in the very last of winter, when every one was in the thick of all the year's tasks and cares, there came to Leonard this letter:--

LEONARD BYINGTON, ESQUIRE:

SIR,--I find myself compelled to ask that you consider your acquaintance-ship with my wife at an end. Doubtless this request will give you more relief than surprise. The visible waste of your frame and the loss of her exquisite bloom are proof enough that both you and she have long been in daily dread of a far worse visitation. It is not worse, because I know how sentimental your impotent and conscience-plagued interchanges of affection have been. I shall permit and assist you to keep this matter a secret. To let it be known would instantly wreck your own career, and would blast at a breath the fortunes of our church and of every one of both our kindreds. I will therefore not at this time require you to resign your church office or to break off those business intimacies with me which, though no longer founded in personal esteem, are vital to interests that common decency must move you to shield from new peril.

I ask for no repair of the inextinguishable wrong you have done me. I only ask you not to fancy that I am to be beguiled by arguments or denials or moved by threats, or that one word I here write is founded on conjecture or inference. Grovelling at my feet, in sobs of shame and with prayers for pardon, Isabel has told me all. Has told me all, Leonard Byington, my once trusted friend. Now, though prostrated on her bed, she rejoices in the double forgiveness of her husband and her priest, blessing him for deliverance from the misleadings of one who--great

God! must I write it?--might at last have dragged her into   crime. It is her request, as it is my command, that you darken our   threshold no more, and that as far as practicable you keep yourself   from her sight.

    Faithfully,
    ARTHUR WINSLOW.

    With his swivel-chair overturned behind him the young lawyer stood at the desk of his inner office, read this letter through at headlong speed, turned it again, and re-read it slowly, searchingly, from his own name to its writer's.

    Then readjusting his chair he stepped to a door, asked a clerk in the outer office to order his cutter, turned back, and was closing his desk, when his partner came to him.

    "Byington, are you ill?" asked the fatherly man.

    "No; I'm only going out on some business. I'll be back about--" He looked at his watch.

    "Byington, don't go. You're ill. You don't realize how ill you are. If you go at all, go home, and let me send some one with you. Why, your hand is as cold"--

    "I'm all right," said the young man, freeing his hand and smiling with white lips. He took his hat and passed out.

    Meanwhile Isabel lay on her bed too overwhelmed to rise. In his room adjoining, with doors locked, Arthur paced the floor. He had spent the first half of the night in an agonizing interview with his wife, and the second half in writing and rewriting the letter to Leonard.

    Now Isabel noticed the cessation of his steps. In the door between them the key turned; then the door opened, and he stood, haggard and dishevelled, gazing on her. She sat up in the bed, wan, tear-spent, her glorious hair falling over the embroideries of her nightdress.

    "Arthur, dear, I am sorry for every angry word I have spoken. But the things I have denied I must deny forever.

    "If you should wait till doomsday, I could confess no more.

    "I have never harbored one throb of unworthy or unsafe regard toward any man in this wide world.

    "For me to say differently would be to lie in God's own face.

"I have had great happiness of Leonard's companionship, and I have been proud to be myself a proof that a man and a woman can be close, dear, daily friends without being lovers or kin, and earth be only more like heaven for it, to them and all theirs. If Leonard has confessed one word more than that for me,--or even for himself, Arthur, dearest,--he has lost his reason. It's a frightful explanation, but I find no other.

"Leonard Byington is not wicked, and if he were he wouldn't be so in a dastard's way.

"Never since the day I first plighted my faith to you, dear heart, has he given me one sign of a lover's love.

"Oh, Arthur, I do love my husband! This night has proved it to me as I never knew it before; and if you will only believe me and go back to Leonard, I believe he can tear the mask off this horrible mystery."

Arthur turned and once more locked the door. His wife flamed red and hearkened, and the light footfall which had tortured her for hours began again. Suddenly she left the bed and hurried to dress.

At the mirror, with her hair lifted on her hands, she paused and again hearkened. Sleighbells stopped at the front door.

Now some one was let in down there, and now, at her husband's room, Giles, his English man of all work, announced Mr. Byington:--

"Yes, sir, but he says if you can't come down 'e will 'ave to come up, sir."

VIII
GIVE YOU FIVE MINUTES

As Arthur entered the library Leonard came from its farther end, and they halted on opposite sides of a large table. Arthur was flushed and looked fearfully spent. Leonard was pale.

"I have your letter, Arthur."

The rector bowed. He gave a start, but tried to conceal a gleam of triumph.

Leonard ignored it and spoke on:--

"A gentleman, Arthur,--I mean any one trying to be a whole gentleman,--is a very helpless creature, nowadays, in matters of this sort."

He looked formidable, and as he lightly grasped a chair at his side it seemed about to be turned into a weapon.

"The old thing once called satisfaction," he continued, "is something one can no longer either ask or offer, in any form. He can neither rail, nor strike, nor spellbind, nor challenge, nor lampoon, nor prosecute."

"Nearly as helpless as a clergyman," said Arthur.

"Almost," replied the visitor. "No, there is no more satisfaction in any of those things, for him, than if he were all a clergyman is supposed to be. There is none even in saying this, to you, here, now, and I'm not here to say it. Neither am I here to vindicate myself--no, nor yet Isabel--with professions or arguments to you; I might as well argue with a forest fire."

"Quite as well. What are you here for?"

"Be patient and I'll tell you; I'm trying to be so with you."

"You--trying"--

"Stop that nonsense, Arthur. Ah me, Arthur Winslow, I have no wish to hu

"Arthur Winslow, I give you five minutes."

miliate you. Through the loyalty of your wife's pure heart, whatever humiliates you must humiliate her. Oh, I could wish her in her shroud and coffin rather than have her suffer the humiliation you have prepared for yourself and for her through you."

Arthur showed a thrill of alarm. "Do you propose to go down to public shame and drag us all with you?"

"No, nor to let you, if I can prevent you. Arthur, you have allowed a base jealousy to persuade you, in the face of every contrary evidence, that your fair young wife has lost her loyalty--and your nearest friend the commonest honesty--in a clandestine love. Under the goadings of that passion you have foully guessed, have heartlessly accused, have brazenly lied. Isabel has confessed nothing to you, and I know by your lies to me how pusillanimously you must have been lying to her. Had your guess been right, I should not have known you were only guessing, and your successful iniquity would have remained hidden from everybody but yourself--I still do you the honor to believe you would have realized it. Now the vital question is, do you realize it, and will you undo it?"

Arthur was deadly pale; his pointing finger trembled. "Leave"--he choked--"leave this house."

Leonard turned scarlet, but his tone sank low. "Arthur, I don't believe your soul is rotten. If I did, I should not be such a knave or such a fool as to make any treaty with you that would leave you in your pulpit one Sabbath Day."

"What do you--what do you mean by that?"

"I mean that such a treaty would be foul faith to everybody."

"So, then, you do propose one common shipwreck for us all."

"Quite the contrary. To trust the fortunes of our loved ones to any treaty with a rotten soul would indeed be to launch them upon a stormy sea in a rotten boat. But I do not believe your soul is so. I believe it is sound,--still sound, though on fire; and so, to help you quench its burning, I give you my pledge to be from this day a stranger to your sweet wife. And now will you do something for me, to prove that your soul is sound and is going to stay sound? It shall be the least I can ask in good faith to the world we live in."

"What is it?" asked Arthur. There was no capitulation in his face or his voice.

"I want you to make to Isabel a full retraction and explanation of every falsehood you have uttered to her or to me in this matter." Leonard was pale again; Arthur burned red a moment, and then turned paler than Leonard.

"You fiend!" gasped the husband. "I am to exalt you, and abase myself, to her?"

"No. No, Arthur. Women are strange; every chance is that in her eyes I shall be abased." The speaker went whiter than ever.

"But be that as it may, you shall have lifted your soul out of the mire. You must do it, Arthur; don't you see you must?"

Arthur sank into the chair at his side. He seemed to have guessed what Leonard was keeping unsaid. A moisture of anguish stood on his brow. Yet--

"I will die before I will do it," he said.

Leonard drew forth the letter, and then his watch. "Arthur Winslow, I give you five minutes. If you don't make me that promise in that time, I shall this day show this letter to your bishop."

The rector sat clenching his fingers and spreading them again, and staring at the table.

A bead of sweat, then a second, and then a third started down his forehead.

Presently he clutched the board, drew himself to his feet, and turned to leave the chair, but fell across its arms, slid heavily from them, and with one rude thump and then another lay unconscious on the floor.

Leonard sprang round the table, but when he would have lifted the fallen head it was in the arms of Isabel, and her dilated eyes were on him in a look of passionate aversion.

"Ring!" she cried. "Ring for Sarah--and go!"

"No! stop! don't ring! he's coming to! Only go! go quickly and forever! Say not a word,--oh, not a word! I heard it all! Despise me too, for I listened at the door!

"Oh, my husband! Arthur, look at me, Arthur. Look, Arthur; it's your Isabel. Oh, Arthur, my husband, my husband!"

IX

THE YOUNG YEAR SMILES

Martin Kelly, pious Irishman and out-door factotum of the Byington place, paused from the last snow-shovelling of the season to reply to a wandering salesman of fruit trees. "Mr. Airthur Winslow or Mr. Linnard Boyington,--naw, sor! ye can see nayther the wan nor th' other, whatsomiver! How can ye see thim, moy graciouz! whin 'tis two weeks since the two o' thim was tuck the same noight wid the pneumonias, boy gorra! and the both of thim has thim on the loongs!"

The nursery agent asked how it had happened so.

"Hawh! ask yer grandmother! All ye can say is they was roipe to catch the maladee, whatsomiver! Ye cannot always tell how 'tis catched, and whin ye cannot tell, moy graciouz! ye have got the wurrst koind!"

The two sick men recovered very nearly at the same time.

One day when Leonard had read all his accumulated mail and had seen three or four men officially in his bedchamber, he told Ruth that a certain criminal case, the trial of which had been waiting for his recovery, would take him to the county-seat, and would keep him there many days, probably weeks, except for brief visits to his office and yet briefer moments at home.

Ruth gave him a look of tender approval, laid a hand in his, and bent into the evening fire her far-off smile. Thus, and only thus, he knew she had divined what had befallen.

A day or two afterward Mrs. Morris brought him a note from Arthur. He wrote an answer while she stayed, and while Ruth listened elatedly to her sprightly account of how well Isabel still bore the burden of nursing a most loving but most nervous husband.

The missive from Arthur was a short but complete and propitiative acknowledgment of his error and fraility. It offered no change in the agreement as to Isabel, but it professed a high yet humble resolve to fall no more, and it ended with a manly offer to resign his pulpit, and even to lay aside his sacred calling, if Leonard retained any belief in the moral necessity of his so doing.

Leonard's reply was a very brief exhortation to his friend to put away all thought of resigning, and to take up his work again with the zeal with which he had first entered upon it.

Mrs. Morris went away refreshed, and left the Byingtons equally so. Her buoyancy had been as prettily restrained, her sympathies as sweet, her dimple as unconscious, her belief in everybody's wit and wisdom except her own as genuine, and her timid dissimulations as kindly meant and as transparent, as ever. Yet there was an unspoken compassion for her when she was gone, for in the parting words with which she playfully vaunted her ignorance of the correspondence she was bearing, it was clear, even to the General, that behind that small ignorance she had a larger knowledge,--a fact that made her dainty cheerfulness seem very brave.

*   *   *   *   *

The freshets swept down the valleys, the myriad yellow twigs of the brookside willows turned green, a cheery piping rose from the ponds, the last gleam of snow passed from the farthest hills, the bluebird sang, the harrow followed the plough, Ruth's crocuses shone above the greening sod, and down by the old mill-pool and on the steep hillside beyond it she and Isabel gathered arbutus, anemones, and the yellow violet. Spring had come.

Then through the thickening greenery the dogwood shone like belated drifts, the flashing warblers passed on into the north, the bobolink had arrived, the robin was already overeating, the whole chorus of birds that had come to nest and stay broke forth, and it was summer.

Leonard was back in his own town, enriched with new esteem from the public and from the men of his profession. The noted case was won, a victory for the peace and dignity of the state, due wholly, it was said, to the energy and sagacity of the young district attorney. A murder had been so cunningly done that suspicion could fasten nowhere, until Byington laid his finger upon a man of so unspotted a name that no one else had had the mental courage to point to him. Through a long and masterly untangling of contradictions the state's counsel had so overwhelmingly proved him guilty that he had confessed without waiting for the jury's verdict.

"Yes," said many, "it was a great stroke, Leonard's management of that thing." And not a few added that it had made him an older man--"that or something." Those who were of his politics, and even some who were not, stopped him in Main Street and State Street to "shake" and to say, without too much care for logical sequence, how soon, in their opinion, he would be the commonwealth's "favorite son."

"My dear Mrs. Morris," said the General, "every town has at least one." But even Mrs. Morris could see the father's faith and pride through the old soldier's satire.

X
THE STORM REGATHERS

On the other hand, things were going ill with the little church of All Angels. Arthur kept his people as tensely strung as ever, but he no longer drew from them the chords of aspiration and enterprise. It was a sad disenchantment, and none the less so because no one seemed to know what the matter was. One darkly guessed he was writing a book, and the vestryman who had praised the lovely simplicity of the wedding lucidly explained that the young rector had "lost his grip."

At times there were flashes of recovery. One Sabbath the whole congregation came out under his benediction uplifted by his word that "loving is living."

"The more we love," they quoted him on their various ways home, "the more we live. The deeper we love, the deeper we live. The more selfishly or unselfishly, the higher, the broader, the purer, the wiser, we love, the more selfishly or unselfishly, the higher, the broader, the purer, the wiser, we live!" The rector's gentle wife was visibly and ever so prettily rejoiced.

True, but hardly the whole truth. In her mother's cottage her smiles were almost sad, and when she had crossed the garden and got into her own room she dropped upon her bed and wept. Yet she quickly ceased, and put on again a brave serenity, for a very tender reason which forbade such risks.

A bunch of the church's best men got together and agreed that all Arthur needed was rest; that this bright moment was the right one in which to offer him a vacation; that his physician should flatly order him to take it; and that Byington should arrange the matter.

Leonard accepted the task, the physician spoke with startling flatness, and the whole kind plot worked well. Arthur consented to go away up into the hills beyond all the jar of the busy world's unrest.

Isabel was to go with him, and they were to sojourn at some point where she would still be within prompt reach of medical skill, yet from which he could make long jaunts into the absolute wilds.

Mrs. Morris was far from well when they left, and the day afterward she was seriously ill. That night Ruth sat up with her, and the next day she was worse, yet begged that no telegram be sent to her daughter.

At the close of the day there came a letter from Isabel. It said that Arthur, "already a new man," would start the next morning at dawn for a three days' trip into the wilderness. He went; and he had not been three hours gone when Isabel received a dispatch calling her to her mother. The only day train would leave in a few minutes, and she had the fortune to catch it.

Ruth met her at the station with the blessed word "better." They went up from the town in Ruth's carriage, Martin Kelly driving, who let it be known that though the doctor's name, "moy graciouz!" were signed to the telegram seven times over, the actual painstaker and sender was "Linnard Boyington, whatsomiver!"

Still Ruth called it the doctor's telegram, and said it made no difference who sent it; but she saw Isabel was disturbed. "Well, Martin, Doctor will have to wait on himself to-morrow; Leonard will be out of town."

That evening, alone with her brother, she said, "But I thought you were to be out of town to-morrow."

"No," he replied, "I don't think I'd better."

Another day passed, another came, and Mrs. Morris was still in danger. Isabel wrote Arthur that she would be with him the moment the peril was over, if he needed her; but if he did not, she would stay on for her mother's fuller recovery. Her letter had barely gone when she received a pencilled line brought in to the mountain hotel by a chance messenger and sent on to her, saying he would be out on his tramp five days instead of three. On the fifth day she telegraphed that her mother was getting well so fast that she would come, now, at his word.

The next morning she betrayed to Ruth a glad sense of relief as she showed her a dispatch from Arthur, which read: "Going on another trip to-morrow. Stay till I write."

Ruth repeated it to her father and brother at their noonday meal. Leonard made no comment, but the General asked pleasantly--

"Is she certain he won't come in on this evening's express?" He was discerning more than any one wanted him to.

However, at dusk came the train, took water at the tank, stopped at the station, and passed on, and Arthur did not appear.

"Well, I'll go to bed," blithely spoke the General. "I'm not so old as I used to be, but I'm tired, after writing that letter this afternoon--to Godfrey. Good-night." So he gave fair notice that he had moved in this matter, himself.

"I didn't know father had received a letter from Godfrey," said Ruth, shading her face from the lamp, and lifting to Leonard a smile which implied that it would have been but fair for him to have told her.

"It came the day before Arthur went away," replied Leonard, and Ruth reluctantly chose a new topic.

They rarely had an evening together thus, and with a soft rain falling at the open windows they sat and talked on many themes in what was to them a very talkative way. When something brought up the subject of the late noted trial, Ruth asked her brother how it had first come to him to suspect so unsuspected a man.

His reply was tardy. "Partly," he said, and mused while he spoke, "because I am so unsuspected a man myself."

He looked up with a smile, half play, half pain. "I know what the mind of an unsuspected man is capable of--under pressure."

The questioner looked on him with fond faith, and then, dropping her eyes to her needlework, said, "That wasn't all that prompted you, was it?"

"No," replied the brother, again musing. "I had noticed the singular value of wanton guesswork."

"I thought so," said the sister. Her needle flagged and stopped, and each knew the other's mind was on the implacable divinations of one morbid soul.

Leonard leaned and fingered the needlework,--a worsted slipper, too small for most men, too large for most women. "Is that for him?"

"Yes," apologized Ruth; "it's the thing every clergyman has to incur. But I'm only doing it to help Isabel out; she has the other."

The evening went quickly. When Leonard let down the window sashes and lowered the shades, Ruth, standing by the lamp as if to put out its light, said, "I'll not go up for a moment or two yet."

She sent him an ardent smile across the room and turned to a desk.

XI
HAS IT COME TO THIS?

Ruth wrote to her lover. Her father's keeping secret his receipt of Godfrey's letter until he had mailed its answer, could mean only that the answer was for Godfrey to come home. The General's talk of being tired by the writing of it was a purely expletive irony, for he had written with the brevity of an old soldier to a young sailor; but he had written that trouble was impending, that its source was Arthur, and that the last hope of removing it lay with him, Godfrey.

A line from Ruth, pursuing after this message, would be one steamer behind it all the way, but it would reach the far wanderer before any leave would permit him to start homeward.

So, now, what should she write? If her father had discerned so much more than he had let any one know he had discerned, how about others? How about the kind whose chief joy is ruthless guesswork? *That* need of haste was one she had overlooked. Wise father!

And yet--haste itself is such a hazardous thing! Ah, if Arthur had come in on that evening express, what to write were an easier question. The minutes sped by; her pen overhung the paper with the opening sentence unfinished, and every moment the thought she kept putting away came back: "Leonard!--Leonard!--Godfrey's summons should go to him from Leonard; and it should flash under the seas, not crawl across them!"--Hark!

She rose and glided to the door through which her brother had gone. There she was startled by the sight of him speeding cautiously down the stair.

*   *   *   *   *

On entering his unlighted room Leonard had moved across it to a front window, where, veiled by the chamber's dusk, he stood looking out into a night dimly illumined by the overclouded moon. The Winslow house widened palely among its surrounding trees. The servants' rooms were remote as well as on the farther side, and on the nearer side no lamplight shone. A short way down the street a glow came from the Morris cottage. Evidently Isabel was with her mother.

He stood and mused, unconsciously lulled by the cool drip of myriad leaves, and with his mind poised midway between emotion and thought. To yield to emotion would have been to chafe against the bands that knitted his life and hers to every life about them. To yield to thought would have been to think of her as no more to be drawn from these surrounding ties than some animate rainbow-fringed flower of the sea can be torn from its shell without laceration and death. To give thought word would have been to cry, "Oh, truest of womankind, where would this unsuspected man, this Leonard Byington, be if you were other than you are?" Yet the suspense between avoided feeling and avoided thought held him where he stood.

So standing, it drifted idly into his mind that yonder arbor must be very wet to-night, and the cinder sidewalk out here much drier. As the thought moved him to draw one step back, the glow from the cottage broadened. Its front door had opened, and Mrs. Morris's young maid came out with a lantern, followed by Isabel saying last fond words to her mother as the convalescent closed the door.

"Good-night!" she called back.

In one great wave the young man's passion rolled over its bounds and brought him to his knees with arms outstretched. "Oh, Isabel!" he murmured. "Oh, my God! Oh, Isabel! Isabel! if I had but lost you fairly!"

The two slight figures came daintily along the wet path in single file, the maid throwing the lantern's beams hither and yon as she looked back to answer Isabel's kindly questions; Isabel one moment half lost in the gloom of the trees, and then so lighted up again from foot to brow that it was easy to see the very lines of her winsome mouth, ripe for compassion or fortitude, yet wishful as a little child's.

Her secret observer moaned as he stood erect. The fury of his soul seemed to enhance his stature. He did not speak again, but, "Oh, Isabel! harder to strive against than all the world beside!" was the unuttered cry that wrote itself upon his tortured brow. "If your unfair winner would only hold you by fair means! Yet I too was to blame! I too was to blame, and you alone were blameless!"

Opposite his window Isabel ceased her light talk with the maid, halted, bent, and scanned something just off the firm path, in the clean wet sand.

The maid turned and flooded her with the light of the lantern just as she impulsively lifted an alarmed glance to Leonard's window and as quickly averted it. "Go on," said the mistress. "I can walk faster if you can."

The girl quickened her steps, but had not taken a dozen when Isabel stopped again. "Wait, Minnie. Now you can run back, thank you." She reached for the lantern.

"I--I thought I was to go all the way, and--and bring the lantern back."

"No, I'll keep the lantern; but I'll stay here and throw the light after you till you get in. Run along."

Minnie tripped away. As she came where they had first halted, a purposely belated good-night softly overtook her; and when she looked back, Isabel, as if by inadvertency, sent the lantern's beam into her eyes. So too much light sent the maid by the spot unenlightened.

Leonard drew aside lest the beam swing next into his window. But the precaution was wasted; the glare followed Minnie.

Isabel also followed, slowly, a few paces, and then moved obliquely into the roadway and toward the window. Only for a moment the ray swept near her unseen observer, and, lighting up the rain-packed sand close before herself, revealed a line of footprints slanting toward her from Leonard's own gate.

As the cottage door shut Minnie in, Isabel, reassured by the brightness of the Byingtons' lower windows, stopped for a furtive instant, and holding in her hand the fellow of the slipper so lately in Ruth's fingers, exactly fitted it to one of these footprints. Then, with the lantern on her farther side, and every vein surging with fright and shame, she made haste toward the open gateway of the Winslow house.

A short space from it she recoiled with a gesture of dismay and self-repression, and her light shone full upon a man. He stepped from the garden, his form tensely lifted, his face aflame with anger.

But her small figure straightened also, and swiftly muffling the lantern in a fold of her skirt, she exclaimed, audibly only to him, though in words clear-cut as musical notes, "Oh, Arthur Winslow, has it come to this?"

She arrested his resentful answer by the uplift of a hand, which left the lantern again uncovered. "Inside! In the house!" she softly cried, starting on. "Not here! Look!--those upper windows!--we're in full view of them!"

Quickly she remuffled the lantern, but not in time to hide his motion as he threw out an arm and pushed her rudely back, while he exclaimed, "In full view of them answer me one question!"

It was then that Leonard went hurriedly downstairs.

XII
THE LANTERN QUENCHED

I will answer you nothing!" murmured Isabel, still facing her husband as she moved round into the garden driveway. "Arthur Winslow, it is you who are on trial, not I!" "I on trial! God, listen to that!"

He sprang after her, gripped her shoulders, and hung over her, snarling, "You two-faced runaway! what have I done but suffer?"

She kept the lantern hid. "What have you done? Oh, my husband, will you hear if I tell you? You have hung the fates of all of us, living or yet to live, on one thread,--please, dear, don't bear so heavily on me,--on one poor thread which the jar of another misstep will surely break. Oh, let us not make it! Come, Arthur,--my husband,--into the house; maybe we can yet save ourselves and our dear ones! Arthur, you're hurting me dreadfully. If you press me down that way, you'll force me to my knees."

Still she spoke in undertone, and still she muffled the light, while steadily the weight of his arms increased. Suddenly he crowded her to the earth. "Arthur," she murmured, "Arthur, what are you going to do? Don't kill me here and now, Arthur; wait till to-morrow. I have that to pass through to-night which may end my life peaceably in bed; and if it should, then there will be no infamy on any of us,--on you or our child, living, or on me, dead; and Godfrey, and Ruth, and mother, and all can be"--

"Give me that lantern!" He held her with one hand, snatched the light from cover, and thrust it into her face. "So this is what you signal him with, is it?"

"Oh no, no! Arthur, dear, no! Before God's throne, no!"

He lifted it as high as his arm would go, and with all his force swung it down, crashing and quenched, upon her head.

She gave a gentle sigh and rolled at his feet. Groaning with horror and fright, he lifted her in his arms and bore her to her room and bed.

There she presently opened her eyes to find him laving her face and head, moaning, covering them with kisses, and imploring her forgiveness in a thousand hysterical repetitions.

"Hush, dear," she whispered. "I see how it all happened. Does anybody know? Oh, God be thanked! don't let any one find out! It was all a misunderstanding. So many things crowded together to mislead you!"

"Oh yes, so many, many things at once, my treasure! Oh yes, yes!"

"Call Sarah, will you, dear?"

"Oh, beloved, why should I? You don't need Sarah for anything."

"Yes, I need her. I must send her for mother--and Ruth--I promised Ruth; and you must send Giles for the doctor; my hour is come."

*   *   *   *   *

In the Byington house Ruth and her brother met at the foot of the stairs.

"Leonard," she whispered, "what is it? Is father ill? Leonard! Oh, what have you seen?"

"Let me pass! quick!" He would have pressed her aside, but she laid hands on him.

"What has Arthur done?" she asked. "What is he doing?"

"Ruth! Ruth! he is putting her out of his own gate!" The brother extended both hands to turn the sister from his path, but she twined her arms on his.

"Leonard! Leonard! for the love of heaven, let him do it! She has only to go to her mother; let her go! It's the last hope. But she'd better be dead, and she'd a hundred times rather be dead, than that Leonard Byington should be her rescuer! Come in here a minute."

Slipping both hands into his she drew him into the lighted room, adding as they went, "In a few minutes I can make some errand to her and find how matters stand"--

They stumbled over a disordered rug. She fell into a chair; he sank to his knees, and with his face in her hands he moaned, "Oh, Ruth! Oh, Ruth! it's my fault after all! I should have gone away at the beginning!"

Ruth and Arthur met face to face in the Winslow garden. "I was just coming for you," he said, excitedly.

"For Isabel?"

"Yes, her mother is with her, and"--a sound of wheels--"here's Giles, now, off for the doctor."

The servant passed. "Yes, I got here by the sunset express. I couldn't stay away--with this impending."

"I didn't see you come."

"No, of course you didn't see me, for I didn't go to the station, and so I didn't pass anywhere near your house. I got off at the tank and came up the hill path."

"You must have got drenched; you *are* drenched."

"Oh no! I got in before the rain began. Let myself in without seeing any one, and found Isabel was over at her mother's. So I waited here."

"Didn't let her know you were home?" asked Ruth, with a penetrating gaze.

"No, I haven't been off the place since I came, but I stepped out so many times into the garden to see if she was coming that I'm soaking wet."

They entered the lighted house, and he turned upon her a glance heavy and wavering with falsehood. His tongue ran like a terrified horse. "Oh--eh--before you go upstairs--Ruth--there's one thing I'm distressed about. I've told Mrs. Morris, and she's promised to see that the doctor understands it perfectly,--though I shall explain it to him myself the moment he comes. And still I wish you'd see that he understands, will you?"

"What is it?"

"Why, at last, as I was waiting for Isabel, and saw her coming, I went to meet her. Unfortunately she took me for a stranger, turned to run, and tripped and fell headlong! She somehow got her lantern between the base of a tree and the crown of her head, smashed the lantern, and cut and bruised her head pitifully!"

To hide her start of distress Ruth moved up the stair; but after a step or two she turned. "Arthur, why say anything about it, if nothing is asked?"

The husband stared at her and turned deadly pale.

"Th--that's tr--true!" he said, with an eager gesture. "I'll not mention it. And--

Ruth!"--she was leaving him--"you might s--say the same to Mrs. Morris!"

She nodded, but would not trust her eyes to meet his. He was right; she had divined his deed.

He went loiteringly into the library and gently closed the door. Then he turned the light low, paced once up and down the room, and all at once slammed himself full length upon a lounge, and lay face up, face down, by turns, writhing and tearing his hair.

Soon again he was pacing the floor, and presently was prone once more, and then once more up.

Giles, his English man, brought the doctor, and Arthur heard him discoursing as the vehicle drew up.

"Yes, sir, quite so; quite so, sir. And yet I believe, sir, if h-all money and lands was 'eld in common, the 'ole 'uman ryce would be as 'appy as the gentlemen and lydies on Bylow 'Ill!"

The young husband met the physician cheerily, sent him up, and went back to his solitude.

An hour passed, and then Sarah Stebbens knocked and leaned in. "Mr. Arthur!"

"What, Sarah?"

"Oh! I didn't see you. All's well, and it's a daughter."

XIII
BABY

It was most pleasant, being asked by everyone, even by General Byington, how it felt to be a grandmother. "Oh! ho, ho!" Mrs. Morris's unutilized dimple kept itself busy to the point of positive fatigue. Even more delightful was it, when the time came round for the totality of her sex--the only sex worth considering--to call and see the babe and mother, to hear them all proclaim it the prettiest infant ever seen, and covertly pronounce Isabel more beautiful than on her wedding day.

In a way she was; and particularly when they fondly rallied her upon her new accession of motherly practical manner, and she laughed with them, and ended with that merry, mellow sigh which still gave Ruth new pride in her and new hope. But another source of Ruth's new hope was that Arthur, who had written to the bishop and resigned his calling the day after Mrs. Morris's little namesake was born, had at length withdrawn his letter.

"It is to your brother we owe its withdrawal," said the bishop, privately, to Ruth.

She beamed gratefully, but did not tell him that, after the long, secret conference between her brother and the rector, Leonard had come to her and wept for Arthur the only tears he had ever shed in her presence. Now Leonard had found occasion to go West for a time, though he still held his office; and Arthur was filling the rectorate almost in the old first way. On some small parish matter the rustic vestryman with the spectacled daughter came to Arthur's library in better spirits than he had shown for months, and by and by asked conjecturally, "I--eh--guess you don't keep any babies here you're ashamed to show, do ye?" and held his mouth very wide open.

The infinitesimal was brought.

"Well, I vum! Why, Miz. Winslow, I don't believe th' ever was a pretty baby so puny, nor a puny baby so pretty! Now, if it's a fair question, I hope y' ain't tryin' to push in between this baby and the keaow, be ye?"

"No," laughed Isabel. "I'm not that conceited. I should only be in the way."

"Well," he said as they parted, shaking Arthur's hand to the end of his speech, "I like to see a baby resemble its father, and that's what this 'n 's a-tryin' to do, jest 's hard 's she can."

So went matters for a time, and then, while the babe began to fill out and lengthen out, Isabel showed herself daily more and more overspent. The physician reappeared, and spoke plainly:--

"And if your cousin down South is so determined to have you at her wedding, why, go! Leave your baby with your mother; she's older in the business than you are."

But the cousin's wedding was weeks away yet, and Isabel clung to her wee treasure, and temporized with the aunts and cousins in the South and with her mother and Ruth at home, until the doctor spoke again.

"Let's see," he said to Arthur. "This is November, baby's five months old. Send your wife away. Put her out! Something's killing her by inches, and I believe it's just care o' the nest. We must drive her off it, as I drove Leonard Byington off,--which, you remember, you, quietly, were the first to suggest to me to do.... Coming back, you say,--Byington? Yes, but only for a day or two,--election time."

It did not occur to the doctor that Arthur was secretly keeping his wife from going anywhere.

The night Leonard came home the old pond, for the first time in the season, froze over, and through Giles's activities it was arranged next day that Martin Kelly, Sarah Stebbens, Minnie, and he should go down there after supper and skate by the light of fagot fires made out on the ice. Giles piled the fagots; but at a late moment, to the disgust of Giles and Minnie, the older pair pitilessly changed their minds, and decided they were too old to make such nincompoops of themselves. Minnie would not go without Sarah, for Minnie was up to her pretty eyebrows in love with Giles, as well as immensely correct; and so there, as it seemed, was the end of that.

At tea Arthur told Isabel he was going for a long walk down through the town and across the meadows, and would not be home before bedtime. Isabel approved heartily, and said Sarah would stay near the sleeping babe, and she would spend the evening with her mother. She and Arthur went together as far as the cross-paths in the arbor, and there, in parting, he clasped and kissed her with a sudden frenzy that only added one more distressful misgiving to the many that now haunted her days.

She found her mother alone. They sat down, hand in hand, before an open fire, and had talked in sweet quietness but a short while, when a chance word and the knowledge that this time they would not be interrupted made it easy for Isabel to say things she had for weeks been trying to say.

XIV
THE TALKATIVE LEONARD

Across the street the father of Leonard and Ruth, already abed, lay thinking of their tribulation and casting about in his mind for some new move that might help to end it happily. Godfrey had not come. He had not looked for him to appear with a hop, skip, and a jump, "a man under authority" as he was; but here were five months gone.

"I can't clamor for him," thought he, and feared Ruth had written him that the emergency was past. And so she had, in those days of new hope and new suspense which had followed for a while Arthur's withdrawal of his resignation.

At the fireside below sat Leonard and Ruth, not hand in hand, like Isabel and her mother, yet conversing on the same theme as they.

Leonard had spent the day at the polls; his party had won an easy victory; and, though not on the ticket, he was now awaiting a telegraphic summons to the state capital. His fortunes were growing. Yet that was not a thing to be wordy about, and now, when the murmur of his voice continued so long and steadily that it found even the dulled ear of the aged father in the upper room, that father knew what the topic must be. On all other matters the son and brother had become more silent than ever,--was being nicknamed far and near, flatteringly and otherwise, for his reticence; but let Ruth sit down with him alone and barely draw near this theme,--this wound,--and his speech bled from him and would not be stanched.

"I can admit I have made the mistake of my life," he said, "but I cannot and will not, even now, give up and say there is nothing to be saved out of it. It's a mistake that has bound me to her, to you, to Godfrey, to him, to all, and demands of me, pinioned and blindfolded as I am, every effort I can make, every device I can contrive, to compel him to free her and you and all of us from this torture.

"He shall not go on eating out our lives. I have dawdled with him weakly, pitifully, but I did it in my hope to save him. I tried to save him for his own sake, Ruth, truly,--as truly as for her sake and ours; and I wanted to save his work with him,--his church, his and hers; so much of it is hers. Oh, Ruth, I love that little bird-box, spite of all its spunky beliefs and twittering complacencies. I wanted to save it and him; and over and over there has seemed such good ground of hope in him. It's been always so unbelievable that he should utterly fail us. Ruth, if you could have seen his contrition the night I tore up that shameful, servile resignation! I don't need to see Isabel to know he is wearing the soul out of her. You needn't have answered one of my questions,--which I honor you for answering so unwillingly; Mrs. Morris gave me their answer in five minutes, though we talked only of investments. And Mrs. Morris needn't have given it; to see Arthur himself is enough. All the genuineness has gone out of the man,--out of his words, out of his face, out of his voice. I wonder it hasn't gone from all of us, driven out by this smirking masquerade into which he has trapped us."

"Have you determined what to do?" asked the sister, gazing into the fire.

"Not yet. But I sha'n't go back West. Flight doesn't avail. And, Ruth"--

"Yes, brother; you've cabled?"

"I have. He'll come at once, this time." A step on the porch drew the speaker to the door.

The telegram from the capital had come. But until its bearer had gone again and was out of hearing down the street the young man lingered in the porch. His mind was wholly on that evening when Isabel had passed with the lantern. Would she pass now? From the idle query he turned to go in, when Ruth came out, and they stayed another moment together. Presently their ear caught a stir at the side of the Morris cottage.

"Hmm," murmured Ruth half consciously, and, with a playful shudder at the cold, whispered, "Come in, come in!"

But then quickly, lest this should carry a hint of distrust, she tripped in alone, closed the door, and glided to the bright hearth. There a moment of waiting changed her mind. She ran again to the door, and began to say as she threw it open, "My brother! you'll catch your"--

But no brother was there.

XV
THE THIN ICE BREAKS

Isabel, who had never confessed her trouble to her mother until now, had this evening told all there was to tell. "No, no, my dear," she said as she moved to go, "I have no dread of his blows. I don't suppose he will ever strike me again. Ah, there's the worst of it; he's got away, away beyond blows. I wish sometimes he'd brain me, if only that would stop his secretly watching me.

"If he'd never gone beyond blows, I would have died before I would have told; not for meekness, dearie, nor even for love,--of you, or my child, or any one,--but just for pride and shame. But to know, every day and hour, that I'm watched, and that every path I tread is full of traps,--there's what's killing me. And I could let it kill me and never tell, if being killed were all. But I tell you because--Oh, my poor little mother dearie, do I wear you out, saying the same things over and over?

"This is all I ask you to remember: that my reason for telling you is to save the honor of my husband himself, and of you, dear heart, and of--of my child, you know. For, mother, every innocent thing I do is being woven into a net of criminating evidence. Sooner or later it's certain to catch me fast and give me over, you and me and--and baby, to public shame."

As they went toward the arbor door Isabel warily hushed, but her mother said: "There's no one to overhear, honey-blossom; Minnie's at your house with Sarah."

But neither was there more to be said. The daughter shut herself out, and stood alone on the doorstep pondering what she had done. For she had acted as well as spoken, and, without knowledge of Leonard's move, was calling Godfrey home herself. Her mother was to send the dispatch in the morning.

So standing and distressfully musing, she heard the click of the Byingtons'

"But to know every day and hour that I'm watched."

door as Ruth left Leonard on the porch. But her thought went after Arthur. Where was he? That he had honestly gone where he had said he was going she painfully doubted. She stirred to move on, but had not taken a step when a feminine cry of terror set her blood leaping and sent her flying down the arbor, and where the two paths crossed she and Leonard met at such a speed that only by seizing her with both his hands did he avoid trampling her down. The scream was repeated again and again.

"It's Minnie!" cried Isabel as they sprang down the path to the mill pond; and Leonard, outrunning her, called back,--

"We'll get her out! She's not gone under!"

The next moment he, and then she, were on the scene. Minnie stood on the firmer ice away from the bank, moaning in continued agitation, but already rescued. It was Arthur Winslow who had saved her.

Now he gained the bank with the dripping girl, where he yielded her to his wife, and without a word from him, from Isabel, or from Leonard to any one but the incessantly talking maid, the four hurried up the path. When they reached the arbor Ruth had joined them, and there the three women turned to the cottage. Leonard passed on toward his home. Arthur went into his own house.

In the cottage, while being hurried into dry clothes, Minnie more coherently explained her mishap. Wishing to play a joke on Giles, she had slipped away from the fireside company of him and Sarah to put a match to his fagots on the pond, run back with word that they were burning, and laugh with Sarah while Giles should plunge out to find the incendiaries. But she had forgotten how frail good ice may be against a warm bank, and leaping down, had promptly broken through. She had had the fortune to hold on by the ice's outer edge until Arthur, whom she felt sure only Providence could have sent there, drew her out. She was tearfully ashamed, yet not so broken in spirit but she fiercely vowed she would get even with Giles for this yet.

Leonard went to his room, Arthur to his, and each in his way shut himself in to darkness, silence, and the fury of his own heart.

One of the things most harrowing to Leonard was that, at every turn, the active part fell to Arthur, while him fate held mercilessly to the passive; and his soul writhed in unworded prayer for any conceivable turn of events that would give him leave to act, to do!

But all he could do was done. Godfrey was sent for: everything must await his coming. Heaven hold Arthur's hand till Godfrey could come!

Ruth returned home and began to lock up the house. When, presently, she tapped at her brother's door and looked in, he had lighted the room and was reading his telegram.

"All right over the way," she said, and to hurry on over the grim untruth repeated briefly Minnie's story. "Good-night. You go--to-morrow? Well, you'll make haste back."

She left him, but later returned.

"Leonard." At the slightly opened door she thrust in her Bible, with a finger on the line, "My soul, wait thou only upon God."

"Thank you," said the brother. "Good-night. I'm afraid we've kept Him waiting on us."

XVI
MUST GIVE YOU UP

Over on the Winslow side of the way, Isabel, having tarried in the cottage to explain to her frightened mother how perfectly natural it was that Arthur, after his tramp across the meadows, should have made a circuit to the upper side of the old mill pool, went pensively home. Presently, holding a lamp, she stood in the door between her room and Arthur's, lifted the light above her head, and, shading her brows, called his name. Hidden in the gloom, silent and motionless, he stared for a moment on the beautiful apparition, and then moved without a sound into the beams of the lamp, a picture of misery and desperation.

"Why in the dark?" amiably inquired the wife.

With widening eyes and spectral motions he drew near.

"In the dark?" he asked. "Why in the dark? The darkness is in me, and all the lamps that light the world's ships into harbor could not dispel it."

All at once he went to his knees. "Oh, my wife, my wife! save me, save me! Hell is in my soul!"

She drew back, and with low vehemence urged him to his feet. "Up! up! My husband shall not kneel to me!"

Laying her hand reverently upon his shoulder she pressed him into his room, set the lamp aside, and let him clasp her wildly in his arms.

"Save me, Isabel," he moaned again. "Save me."

"From what, dear heart,--from what can I save you?" She drew him to a seat and knelt beside him.

"From the green-eyed demon that has gnawed, gnawed, gnawed at my heart till it is rent to shreds, and at my brain--my brain!--till it is almost gone." His brow drooped to hers. "Almost gone, beloved; my brain is almost gone."

"No, Arthur, dearest, no, no, no; your heart is torn, but your mind, thank God, is whole. This is only a mood. Come, it will pass with one night's sleep."

Still he held her brow beneath his. "Save me, Isabel; my soul is almost gone. Oh, save me from the fiends that come before me and behind me, by night and by day, eyes shut or eyes open."

"My husband! my love! how can I save you? How can I help you? Tell me how."

"Hear me! hear me confess! That will save me, oh, so sweetly, so sweetly! That will save me from the faces--the white, white faces that float on that black pool down yonder, and move their accusing lips at me: *his* face--and mine--and thine. Oh, Isabel, until you stood before me in the golden light of your lamp, transfigured into a messenger from heaven, it was in my lost soul to do the deed this night."

The wife laid her palms upon her husband's temples, and putting forth her strength lifted them and looked tenderly into his eyes.

"Dear heart, you do not frighten me. You know how unaccountably fear deserts me in fearful moments. But I know there's nothing for either of us to fear now. This is all in your tortured imagination, and there, though you had not seen me, it would have stayed; you never would have come to the act. Arthur, your soul is not lost. You who have pointed the way of escape and deliverance so clearly and savingly to so many, you need not miss it now yourself."

"Idle words, Isabel,--idle, idle words. The very words of Christ are idle to me until I give you up."

"Give me up, my husband? Dear love, you cannot! You shall not! I will not be given up. You haven't the cause, and I haven't the cause."

"Oh, Isabel, I stole you! And the curse of God has gone with the theft, and with every step of the thief, from the first day till now. From the first day until now God has lifted that other man up and brought me down. And yet, before God who said, Thou shalt not covet thy neighbor's wife, he loves you this moment--now!--with the love of a man for a woman."

"Arthur, no! If he did"--

"Isabel, if he did not--if he did not love you yet as before he lost you--oh! if he did not love you infinitely more now than then--he would not be Leonard Byington. That is all my evidence, all my argument, all the ground of my hate; and I hate him with a hatred that has finished--finished!--with my heart, and is devouring my brain."

"Oh, my poor husband, listen to"--

"Listen to me!" he broke in. "Listen before I lose the blessed impulse to say there is but one cure. I must give you up to Leonard Byington. Oh, let me speak! I took you from him by law; by law I will give you back."

"Do you mean divorce, Arthur?"

"I do."

"On what ground?"

"On the ground of ill treatment. You shall bring suit; I will plead guilty."

She rose, with his temples still in her hands. "Ah! whose words are idle now?"

She bent over him with eyes of passionate kindness. "You did not take me from him. You asked me to take you, and for better for worse, till death us do part, I took you, Arthur, knowing as much of any other man's love for me as I know at this hour. You could not steal me; the shame would be mine, to have let you. You are no thief! I am no stolen thing! You shall be happy with me; you shall not give me up!"

He leaped to his feet and snatched her into his arms. The babe cried sleepily from its mother's room. She tenderly disengaged herself, left him in the door, moved on to the child's crib, and in the dim light of the bedside taper, facing him from beyond it, soothed the little one by her silent touch.

To Arthur, wan and frail though she was, the sight was heavenly fair, a vision of ineffable peace to which it seemed a sacrilege to draw nearer; but she beckoned, and he stole to the spot. With the quieted babe in its crib between them, the pair knit arms about each other's neck and kissed.

"My own! my own at last!" murmured the husband. "I never had you until now!"

"The cure has worked, dear heart," breathed the wife,--"worked without surgery, has it not?"

"The cure has worked," he replied,--"worked without the sacrifice. Oh, the sudden sweet ease of it!" Whispering a fervent good-night in response to hers, he covered her head and brows with caresses; then stole away with eyes still fastened on her, and at the dividing threshold waved a last parting and closed the door.

XVII
SLEEP, OF A SORT

Isabel went to her couch in great heaviness and agitation. Her sad confidings to her mother, Minnie's adventure, Arthur's pitiful if not alarming condition, she strove to reconsider duly and in their order; but perpetually there interfered, with its every smallest detail thrillingly clear and strong, that moment which had thrown her once more into the company, tossed her into the very clutch, of Leonard Byington. She turned her face into her pillow and prayed God for other thoughts and visions, and at length, while charging herself to see her mother in time to postpone the sending of her dispatch to Godfrey, she slept.

Sleep, of a sort, came also to Arthur, though not before many an evil imagination had come back to tease and sting his galled mind.

What chafed oftenest was the fact that Isabel, had he allowed it, would have sought to argue down his belief that Leonard loved her. Great heaven! what must be her feeling toward him, that she should offer to argue such a question? She might truly deny all knowledge of his passion, but oh, where were her quick outcries of womanly abhorrence? Where was the word that Leonard Byington was no more to her than any other man,--that word which would have been the first to flash from her if conscience had not stopped it? Twice he sprang up in his bed, whispering: "They love! They love! Each knows it of the other! They love!"

The second time, as he stared, suddenly he saw them! They stood just beyond the foot of his couch, wrapped in each other's arms. Choking with wrath, freezing with horror, he slid to the floor; but at his first step they floated apart. Isabel glided toward her own door, fading as she went, and dissolved in a broad moonbeam. Leonard, as he receded, grew every instant more real, until, at his pursuer's second step, he melted through a window and was gone. Arthur sprang to the spot and stared out and down; but all he saw was the moon, the frosty night, and the silent, motionless garden.

With a whisper of fierce purpose he turned and noiselessly threw on his clothes, then clutched his head in his hands in a wild effort to recall what the purpose was, and by and by lay quietly down again on his bed. He could not recollect; but the inner tumult quieted more and more, and after a time, without putting off any part of his dress, he drew the bedcovers over himself, and in a few moments was partially asleep. So for an hour or more he lay in half-waking dreams, ghastly with phantoms and breathless with dismay of his own ferocious strivings. Then he rose once more, and, with the noiselessness which habit had perfected, left his room, moved down the upper hall and the stair, and let himself out into the garden. Wadded in his arms he bore one or two of the coverings from his bed. He took his way to the pond.

He was walking in his sleep.

At an earlier day Isabel would have been awakened by her husband's softest movement; but now, used to his stirrings, weary in body and mind, and in some degree reassured, she slept on unstartled until Arthur's return.

He came as silently as he had gone, and was empty-handed. He had tied a great stone in the two bed-coverings, and through the thin new ice of the hole where Minnie had broken in had sunk them in the black depth under the shelving rock. He was still asleep.

The door between the two chambers gave a faint sound as he opened it, yet neither mother nor child moved. A moment passed, and he had reached the bed. Another went by, and Isabel was awake, wildly but vainly trying to scream, to rise. A knee was on her bosom, two hands grappled her throat, and two out-starting eyes were close to hers. Her husband was strangling her.

Then he too awoke. With a horrified cry he recoiled, and she, for the first time in her life in a transport of terror, hurled him, in the strength of her frenzy, to the farther side of the bed, and writhing out on the opposite side, crept under it and lay still. In a torture of bewilderment and remorse Arthur buried his face in the bedside. Then, helpless to distinguish what he had done from what he had dreamed, he sprang back to the place where Isabel had lain sleeping, and lo, it was empty.

"Oh, was it thou, was it thou?" he wailed, in a stifled voice. "Was it not he?"

Whispering and moaning her name, hearkening and groping, he sought her from corner to corner, first of her room and then of his own, and then went to the hall and to other rooms in the same harrowing quest.

Isabel crept forth and darted to her babe. Yet as she leaned to take it in her arms her better judgment told her the child was safe. The husband too, and every one beside, were safer from his jealous wrath while the babe remained. With one anguished knitting of her hands over it she left it, and fled in her night-dress. Arthur's course was made plain by his moanings, and easily avoiding him, she glided down a back stair, out into the arbor, and across to her mother's cottage and bed-chamber. As she did so he returned hurriedly to his room, with low cries of less wretched conviction, and looked eagerly under his bed and then under hers. Thereupon the last hope died, and he dropped to his face on the floor in abject agony.

XVIII
MISSING

After a time a new conjecture brought him to his feet. To solve it he would go to the pond. If he had truly been there and done this appalling thing, he would know it by the empty imprint of the boulder he had taken from its resting place of years. If he had not, then Isabel had fled to her mother and would be found with her in the morning, and the blot of her murder, though it blackened his soul, was yet not on his hands.

He went to the water, and soon he came again with the step and face of one called out of his grave. Slowly he counted the disordered coverings of his wife's couch, stood a moment in desolate perplexity, and then went quickly and counted those of his own. A sheet and a blanket were gone. He turned to a closet and supplied the lack, and then paced the floor until dawn.

Before the servants were fairly astir he laid away the clothing Isabel had put off, and contrived to leave the house and pass through the arbor unseen until he reached its farther end; but there Mrs. Morris, in a dressing gown, opened to him before he could knock. She forced her usual laugh, but he saw the white preparedness of her face.

"She knows my crime," he thought, and was in agony to guess how she had got the knowledge and what she would do with it.

"Why, Arthur," she sweetly began, "what brings you"--But her throat closed.

"Mother," he interrupted emotionally as they shut themselves in, "is Isabel here?"

"Isabel?--No-o! Why--why, Arthur, she went home last night before ten o'clock!" The little lady knew her acting was not good, but it was better than she had hoped to make it. "Arthur Winslow! don't tell me my child is not at home! Oh, my heavens!"

"Wait, mother; listen. I beseech you. Do you absolutely know she's not here?"

"I know it! Oh, Arthur, are you only trying to break bad news to me by littles? Has Isabel destroyed herself? Has she fled?" The inquirer played well now; her pallor, that had seemed to accuse him, was gone, and her question offered a cue which he greedily took.

"Fled? Isabel! Destroyed herself,--that spotless soul? Oh no, no, no! But Oh merciful God! I am afraid she has been stolen!" He sank into a seat and dropped his face into his hands.

The maid's steps sounded overhead, and he started up. Mrs. Morris laid a hand on his arm. She was pale again, but her words were reassuring.

"It's Minnie," she murmured: "let me go and see her. She'll not be surprised; I'm always the first one up." She went, and was soon back again.

"There is no time to lose"--Arthur began.

"No, you must go. Go search for every clue that will tell us a word of her; but, whatever you do, let no one, not even Sarah, know she is missing, until we know enough ourselves to protect her from every shadow of reproach!"

"True! true! right! right!" said Arthur, while with secret terror he cried to himself: "This woman knows! She knows, she knows, and all this is make-believe, put on to gain time!"

But he saw no safer course than to help on the sham. "Right," he said again; "only, mother, dear, how shall we hide her absence?"

"We needn't hide it. You know she got another telegram last night, begging her to come at once to the wedding. We can say she went on this morning's train, before day; it makes such good Southern connections. And now go! make your search with all your might! and after a while I'll come over and pack a trunk full of her things, and express it South, just as if she were there, and had gone so hurriedly that--Don't you see?"

Arthur said he saw it all, but he did not; he saw much that was not, and much that was he saw not. He did not see that the dust of the old street, and of the new town as well, was on Mrs. Morris's shoes; and that Isabel, in a gown which she had left at the cottage when she went to be mistress of his home, was really on the train, bound South.

Dropping all pretence of having any search to make, he hurried back to his own room, and by and by told the pleasantly astonished Sarah and Giles the simple truth as Mrs. Morris had put it into his mouth, but told it in the firm belief that he was covering a hideous crime with an all but transparent lie.

After a false show of breakfasting he went into his study,--"to work on his sermon," he said; but did nothing there but pace the floor, hold his head, and whisper, "It will not last an hour after *he* has heard it," and, "O God, have mercy! Oh, my wife, my wife! Oh, my brain, my brain!"

XIX
A DOUBLE STILL HUNT

Mrs. Morris's task was too large for her. She had always taken such care of her innocence that her cultivation of the virtues had been only incidental. Hence, morally, she had more fat than fibre; and hence again, though to her mind guilt was horrible, publicity was so much worse that her first and ruling impulse toward any evil doing not her own was to conceal it. That was her form of worldliness, the only fault she felt certain she was free from. And here she was, without a helping hand or a word of counsel, laboring to hide from the servants and from the dear Byingtons, from the church and from a scoffing world, the hideous fact that Isabel was a fugitive from the murderous wrath of a jealous husband, and that the rector of All Angels had crumbled into moral ruin.

"And oh," she cried, "is it the worst of it, or is it the best of it, that in this awful extremity he keeps so sane, so marvellously sane?" She said this the oftener because every few hours some new sign to the contrary forced itself upon her notice. Oblivion was her cure-all.

For a while after his conference with Mrs. Morris Arthur made some feeble show--for her eye alone--of looking after clews, and then, as much to her joy as to her amazement, told her it was a part of his detective strategy to return into his study, and seemingly to his ordinary work, until time would allow certain unfoldings for which he looked with confidence.

"Have you found out anything?" she asked, with a glaringly false eagerness that gave him a new panic of suspicion and whetted his cunning.

He said he had, but must beg her not to ask yet what it was. Then he inquired if any neighbor had left town that morning for Boston, and her heart rose into her throat as she marked the subtlety he could not keep out of his dark face.

"Why, ye--yes--n--no, no one that I know of ex--except Leonard Byington," she replied, and thought, "If he should accuse Leonard, we are undone!"

To avoid that risk she would have told him, then and there, all she knew, had she not feared she might draw his rage upon herself for aiding the wife's flight. She must, must, must keep on good terms with him till she and Isabel could somehow get the child. So passed the awful hours, mother and husband each marvelling in agony over the ghastly puzzle of the other's apathy.

Later in the day she knocked timorously at his study door. She had come with a silly little proposition that he let her take the infant and go South as if to join Isabel. Thus the trunk would not lie in the express office down there, unclaimed and breeding awkward inquiries, and she from that point, with him at this, could keep up the illusion they had invented until Isabel herself should--eh--return!

But when he let her in, he stood before her a silent embodiment of such remorse and foreboding that she could have burst into sobs and cries.

Yet she broached her plan, trembling visibly, while he heard her through with melancholy deference.

In reply he commended it, but called to her notice how much better it would be for her to go alone. Then the babe, left behind, would be an unspoken yet most eloquent guarantee that its mother would soon reappear.

"Very true," responded the emboldened lady; "yet on the other hand"--

He put out an interrupting touch. "The child is as safe with me as if it were in its mother's bosom."

"Oh, it isn't so much a question of safety as"--

The father interrupted again, with a gleam in his eyes like the outflashing of a knife. "I hold the child against all comers, and would if I had to slay its mother to do it."

Mrs. Morris stifled an outcry and would have left him, but he would not let her.

"Stay! Oh, listen to a soul in torment! The babe is already motherless. Isabel can never return, mother; she is with the dead. I am not waiting idly here for her; I am waiting busily--for her slayer. He has fled; but when he sees he is not pursued

"I am waiting busily for her slayer."

he will come back to the spot,--to the black, black hole. He cannot help it. I *know* that. Oh, how well I know it! And the moment he comes he is caught,-- caught in the web of proofs I am weaving!"

He held her arm and gazed into her gazing eyes in ferocious fear of the web she might be weaving for him; while she, reeling sick with fear of him, tried with all her shaken wits to sham an impassioned accord.

"And you *will* wait?" she exclaimed approvingly. "You will not stir till the thing is sure?"

He would not stir till the thing was sure.

As soon as it was dark enough to slip over to the Byingtons' unseen, she went, bearing to Ruth Isabel's apologetic good-bys, trying her small best to play at words with the General, and quickly getting away again, grateful for a breath of their atmosphere, though distressfully convinced that Ruth had divined the whole trouble, through the joy betrayed by herself on hearing that Leonard would be away for a week.

She went home and slept like a weary child, and neither the next day nor the next, nor the next, was so awful as this first had been; they lacked the crackle and glare, and the crash, of the burning and falling temple.

XX
A DOUBLE RETURN

Let us not attempt the picture of Isabel keeping the happy guise of a wedding guest among her kindred and childhood playmates while her heart burned with perpetual misery, yearning, and alarm. "My baby, my baby!" cried her breast, while the babe slept sweetly under faultless care.

Nor need we draw a close portrait of her husband's mind, if mind it could longer be called. A horror of sleep, a horror of being awake and aware, remorse, phantoms, voices, sudden blazings of wrath as suddenly gone, sweating panics, that craven care of life which springs so rank as the soul decays, and a steady, cunning determination to keep whole the emptied shell of reputation and rank,--these were the things that filled his hours by day, by night; these, and a frightful expectance of one accusing, child-claiming ghost that never came. The air softened to Indian summer; the ice faded off the pool; a million leaves, crimson and bronze, scarlet and gold, dropped tenderly upon its silvering breadth and lay still; and both the joyless master of the larger house and the merry maid of the cottage asked Heaven impatiently if the pond would never freeze over again.

It was Saturday afternoon when Giles, asked by Sarah Stebbens where Mr. Arthur was, told her he was again, as he had been so many times the last three days, down by the water, sitting at the edge of the overhanging bank; or, as the Englishman expressed it, "'dreamink the 'appy hours aw'y.'" So the week passed out; a second came in, and the rector of All Angels went to his sacred office.

He knew, before he appeared in the chancel, that Mrs. Morris was in her accustomed place, and Ruth and her father in theirs, and that Leonard was not yet reported back nor looked for; but exactly as he began to read, "'Dearly beloved brethren, the Scripture moveth us, in sundry places, to acknowledge and confess our manifold sins and wickedness, and that we should not dissemble nor cloak them before the face of Almighty God our heavenly Father'"--a sickness filled Mrs. Morris's frame, a deathly hue overspread the minister's face, and Leonard came in and sat beside his father and sister.

Yet the service went on. The people knelt.

"'Almighty and most merciful Father; We have erred, and strayed from thy ways like lost sheep. We have followed too much the devices and desires of our own hearts'"--

Thus far the rector's voice had led, but here it sank, and the old General's, in a measure, took its place.

Then it rose again, in the confession, "There is no health in us," and in the supplication, "Have mercy upon us, miserable offenders."

There once more it failed, while the people, faltering with distress, repeated, "That we may hereafter lead a godly, righteous, and sober life, To the glory of thy holy Name. Amen."

At this the farmer with the spectacled daughter stepped nimbly over the rail and caught Arthur as he rose and staggered. Leonard was hurrying forward, and half the people kneeling, half standing, when Mrs. Morris vacantly stopped his way with a face so aghast and words so confused that he had to give her over to Ruth. Then he hastened on to where Arthur was being led into the vestry by his physician and others.

But now he was turned back by the doctor, requesting him to dismiss the congregation; which he did, with the physician's assurance that the trouble was no more than vertigo, and that Arthur was even now quite able to proceed home in the farmer vestryman's rockaway. The people noticed that the physician went with him.

Mrs. Morris followed on foot with the farmer's daughter, and with Ruth and the General, and Leonard went into town to telegraph Isabel, in her mother's name, to come home. As he was starting, Mrs. Morris drew Ruth aside and whispered something about Godfrey. To which Ruth softly replied, with an affectionate twist in her smile, "It couldn't hurry him; he's already on the way."

In the room next that in which her son-in-law lay asleep under anodynes the

little mother's odd laugh was turned all to moan. "Oh!--ho--ho!" she sighed in solitude, "if Arthur could have learned from Godfrey how to wait, or even if Isabel
could but have learned from Ruth how to keep one waiting!"

She paused at a window that looked over the garden and into the street. Leonard
passed. She turned quickly away, only sighing again, "Oh!--ho--ho!" Her thought
might have been kinder had she known he was stabbing himself at every step with
blame of all this woe.

"I ought to have foreseen," was his constant silent cry. "I am the one who ought
to have foreseen."

Lack of Sunday trains and two failures to connect kept Isabel from arriving until nightfall of the third day, Wednesday. Arthur knew Mrs. Morris had telegraphed
for her; but to him that was only part of the play under which he thought he and
she were hiding the frightful truth.

On this day he had so outwitted his village physician as to be given the freedom
for which he ravened; liberty to take the air in his garden, as understood by the
doctor, but by him liberty to stand guard down at the edge of that dark pool which
would not freeze over,--liberty to take an air sweet with the odors of the parting
year, but crowded also with distended eyes and strangling groans.

He was down there in the early starlight when Ruth drove softly into the garden, bringing Isabel. Warily the mother came out into the pillared porch, and silently received the house's mistress into her arms.

"He doesn't know," she said. "I couldn't tell him till you should come, for fear
of disappointing him." The argument seemed strained, but no one said so, and with
a whispered good-night Ruth drove away, and the two went in. As they stole upstairs they debated how Isabel had best reveal herself. "I'm terribly afraid that won't
work, blessing," said Mrs. Morris; "you'd better let me break it to him, first."

"No, dearie, I don't think so. I haven't the shadow of a fear"--

"Oh, my darling child, you never have!"

"But I know him so well, mother. We have only to come unexpectedly face
to face and--Oh, I've seen the effect so often!" They entered her room whispering:
"I'll change this dress for the one he last saw me in, and stand over here by the crib
where I stood then, and--Oh, sweet Heaven! is this my little flower sleeping just as
I left her?" With clasped hands and tearful eyes she bent over the child.

XXI
EVENING RED

Then she began to unrobe, but stopped to throw her arms about her mother's neck. "Now, dearly beloved, you hurry away down the path and persuade him up and send him in. I'm only afraid you'll find him chilled half to death, it's growing cold so fast. And you can follow in after him, dearie, if you wish,--only not too close."

The mother went, and had got no farther than the cross-path when she came all at once upon the master of the house.

"Oh! ho, ho! here you are! I was just--Arthur, dear, where is your overcoat? Do go right up to your room, my son, till I can get Sarah to have a fire started in the library." She multiplied words in pure affright, so drawn was his face with anguish, and so wild his eyes with aimless consternation.

Without reply he passed in and went upstairs. Mrs. Morris remained below.

Isabel's heart beat fast. She had made her change of dress, and in a far corner of her room, with her face toward the open door that let into his, was again leaning with a mother's ecstasy over the sleeping babe, when she heard his step.

It came to his outer door, which from her place could not be seen.

Did he stop, and stand there? No, he had not stopped; he was only moving softly, for the child's sake.

She stood motionless, listening and looking with her whole soul, and wishing the light were less dim in this shadowy corner, but knowing there was enough to show her to him when he should reach the nearer door. The endless moment wore away, and there on the threshold he stood--if that--Oh merciful God!--if that was Arthur Winslow.

"Arthur! Arthur! can't you speak?"

His eyes fell instantly upon her, yet he made neither motion nor sound, only stayed and stared, while an unearthly terror came into his face.

Care of the child kept her silent, but in solemn tenderness she lifted her arms toward him.

He uttered a freezing shriek and fled. In an instant his tread was resounding in the hall, then on two or three steps of the stair as she hurried after, and then there came a long, tumbling fall, her mother's wail in the hail below, and a hoarse cry of dismay from Giles as he rushed out of the library.

"He's only stunned, mum," Giles was saying as Isabel reached the spot. "He's no more nor just stunned, mum."

He had lifted the fallen man's head and shoulders, and Mrs. Stebbens came, dropping to her knees and sprinkling water into the still, white face.

Isabel threw herself between.

"Arthur! Arthur! can't you speak? Oh, let us move him into the library!"

"Yes, um!" exclaimed Giles. "'E'll come to in there; you can see 'e's only stunned."

He tried to raise him, and Isabel and Sarah moved to help; but the wife turned on hearing Ruth's voice at her side, and Leonard Byington lifted the limp man in his arms unaided, and bore him to the library lounge.

"Arthur," he pleaded, with arms still under him, "can't you speak to us, dear boy? Say at least good-by, can't you, Arthur?" He parted the clothing from neck and breast, and laid an ear to his heart.

"Do you hear it, Leonard?" cried the wife. "Oh, you do hear it, don't you, Leonard?"

There was no answer. For a moment Leonard's own form relaxed, and he turned his face and buried it in the unresponsive breast. Then he lifted it again, and taking the other face between his hands he sank his brow to the brow upturned and cried: "God rest your soul, Arthur! Oh, Arthur, Arthur, God rest your soul!"

XXII
MORNING GRAY

Mrs. Morris gave the physician her account of the accident, the physician gave the reporters his, and no other ever got into the old street or the town it looks down upon with such sweet superiority. Said the rustic vestryman to another pall-bearer, as they turned toward their homes, "Many's the time All Angels's been craowded, but I never see it craowded as 'twas this time."

The new mound was white under January snows when Godfrey and Isabel first stood beside it together; and when summer had come and gone again, and at last the time drew near when, by the regular alternations of the service, the ocean wanderer's three years afloat were to be followed by three ashore, it was beside that mound that Ruth let him ask the long-withheld question.

And once more the new year followed the old.

On one of its earliest days, "I cal'late," a certain somebody began to say to General Byington, "th' never was a happier weddin' so quiet, nor a qui--" But he caught the sheen of his daughter's spectacles and forebore.

And still moved on the heavenly procession of the seasons; and as each new one passed with smile and song, and strewed its flowers or fruits on Bylow Hill, the memory of one who after life's fitful fever slept soundly at last was ever a sweet forgetting of all that had once been bitter, and a sweeter and sweeter remembrance of whatsoever things had been pure, lovely, and of good report.

One day the travelling salesman of fruit trees came again. This time he met Minnie, some of whose information puzzled him.

"But I thought you said the young Mrs. Winslow lived in the large house on this side."

"Yes, but that's the other one; that's Mrs. Isabel Winslow, the widow. Captain Winslow, he's so much o' the time to the navy yard that him and his wife they just keep their home along with her father and Mr. Leonard."

"And who is it that, I understand, a Mr. Giles over here is about to marry?"

For reply Minnie covered her mouth and nose with her hand, sputtered, and shut the door in his face.

Another year went by, yet another followed, and still Ruth--daughter, sister, wife, and mother--remained the happy mistress of the house in which she was born, and Leonard remained one of her household. Mrs. Morris turned the cottage over to Mr. and Mrs. Giles--hem!--and dwelt in the Winslow house with Isabel; who, even the young said, grew more beautiful and lovable all the time.

But there came a day, after all,--year uncertain,--when Leonard, with Mrs. Morris's little namesake on his knee, asked Isabel if she did not think it would be well for him to go away for a while; and Isabel murmured no.

So by and by the Winslow pair went to live in the Winslow house, and the Byington pair in the Byington house; and if you listen well, you may hear an aged voice, a voice with a brogue, saying:--

"Ay! there's a Linnard Winslow, now, and there's a Godfrey Boyington. And there's still an Isable Winslow and a Ruth Boyington. But the mother of Ruth Boyington is she that wor Isable Winslow, moy graciouz! and the mother of Isable Winslow is she that wor Ruth Boyington. And so there be's an Isable in the wan house and an Isable in th' other; and there be's a Ruth in the wan house and a Ruth in th' other, moy graciouz! and there's an Airthur in each, whatsomiver!"

The Codes Of Hammurabi And Moses
W. W. Davies

QTY

The discovery of the Hammurabi Code is one of the greatest achievements of archaeology, and is of paramount interest, not only to the student of the Bible, but also to all those interested in ancient history...

Religion   ISBN: *1-59462-338-4*   Pages:132
MSRP $12.95

The Theory of Moral Sentiments
Adam Smith

QTY

This work from 1749. contains original theories of conscience amd moral judgment and it is the foundation for systemof morals.

Philosophy ISBN: *1-59462-777-0*   Pages:536
MSRP $19.95

Jessica's First Prayer
Hesba Stretton

QTY

In a screened and secluded corner of one of the many railway-bridges which span the streets of London there could be seen a few years ago, from five o'clock every morning until half past eight, a tidily set-out coffee-stall, consisting of a trestle and board, upon which stood two large tin cans, with a small fire of charcoal burning under each so as to keep the coffee boiling during the early hours of the morning when the work-people were thronging into the city on their way to their daily toil...

Pages:84

Childrens   ISBN: *1-59462-373-2*   *MSRP $9.95*

My Life and Work
Henry Ford

QTY

Henry Ford revolutionized the world with his implementation of mass production for the Model T automobile. Gain valuable business insight into his life and work with his own auto-biography... "We have only started on our development of our country we have not as yet, with all our talk of wonderful progress, done more than scratch the surface. The progress has been wonderful enough but..."

Pages:300

Biographies/   ISBN: *1-59462-198-5*   *MSRP $21.95*

The Art of Cross-Examination
Francis Wellman

QTY

I presume it is the experience of every author, after his first book is published upon an important subject, to be almost overwhelmed with a wealth of ideas and illustrations which could readily have been included in his book, and which to his own mind, at least, seem to make a second edition inevitable. Such certainly was the case with me; and when the first edition had reached its sixth impression in five months, I rejoiced to learn that it seemed to my publishers that the book had met with a sufficiently favorable reception to justify a second and considerably enlarged edition. ..

Pages:412

Reference   **ISBN: *1-59462-647-2***   *MSRP $19.95*

On the Duty of Civil Disobedience
Henry David Thoreau

QTY

Thoreau wrote his famous essay, On the Duty of Civil Disobedience, as a protest against an unjust but popular war and the immoral but popular institution of slave-owning. He did more than write—he declined to pay his taxes,   and was hauled off to gaol in consequence. Who can say how much this refusal of his hastened the end of the war and of slavery ?

Law   **ISBN: *1-59462-747-9***   **Pages:48**

MSRP $7.45

Dream Psychology Psychoanalysis for Beginners
Sigmund Freud

QTY

Sigmund Freud, born Sigismund Schlomo Freud (May 6, 1856 - September 23, 1939), was a Jewish-Austrian neurologist and psychiatrist who co-founded the psychoanalytic school of psychology. Freud is best known for his theories of the unconscious mind, especially involving the mechanism of repression; his redefinition of sexual desire as mobile and directed towards a wide variety of objects; and his therapeutic techniques, especially his understanding of transference in the therapeutic relationship and the presumed value of dreams as sources of insight into unconscious desires.

Pages:196

Psychology   **ISBN: *1-59462-905-6***   *MSRP $15.45*

The Miracle of Right Thought
Orison Swett Marden

QTY

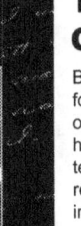

Believe with all of your heart that you will do what you were made to do. When the mind has once formed the habit of holding cheerful, happy, prosperous pictures, it will not be easy to form the opposite habit. It does not matter how improbable or how far away this realization may see, or how dark the prospects may be, if we visualize them as best we can, as vividly as possible, hold tenaciously to them and vigorously struggle to attain them, they will gradually become actualized, realized in the life. But a desire, a longing without endeavor, a yearning abandoned or held indifferently will vanish without realization.

Pages:360

Self Help   **ISBN: *1-59462-644-8***   *MSRP $25.45*

QTY

The Rosicrucian Cosmo-Conception Mystic Christianity *by Max Heindel* ISBN: *1-59462-188-8* **$38.95**
The Rosicrucian Cosmo-conception is not dogmatic, neither does it appeal to any other authority than the reason of the student. It is: not controversial, but is: sent forth in the, hope that it may help to clear.. New Age/Religion Pages 646

Abandonment To Divine Providence *by Jean-Pierre de Caussade* ISBN: *1-59462-228-0* **$25.95**
"The Rev. Jean Pierre de Caussade was one of the most remarkable spiritual writers of the Society of Jesus in France in the 18th Century. His death took place at Toulouse in 1751. His works have gone through many editions and have been republished... Inspirational/Religion Pages 400

Mental Chemistry *by Charles Haanel* ISBN: *1-59462-192-6* **$23.95**
Mental Chemistry allows the change of material conditions by combining and appropriately utilizing the power of the mind. Much like applied chemistry creates something new and unique out of careful combinations of chemicals the mastery of mental chemistry... New Age Pages 354

The Letters of Robert Browning and Elizabeth Barret Barrett 1845-1846 vol II ISBN: *1-59462-193-4* **$35.95**
by Robert Browning and Elizabeth Barrett Biographies Pages 596

Gleanings In Genesis (volume I) *by Arthur W. Pink* ISBN: *1-59462-130-6* **$27.45**
Appropriately has Genesis been termed "the seed plot of the Bible" for in it we have, in germ form, almost all of the great doctrines which are afterwards fully developed in the books of Scripture which follow... Religion/Inspirational Pages 420

The Master Key *by L. W. de Laurence* ISBN: *1-59462-001-6* **$30.95**
In no branch of human knowledge has there been a more lively increase of the spirit of research during the past few years than in the study of Psychology, Concentration and Mental Discipline. The requests for authentic lessons in Thought Control, Mental Discipline and... New Age/Business Pages 422

The Lesser Key Of Solomon Goetia *by L. W. de Laurence* ISBN: *1-59462-092-X* **$9.95**
This translation of the first book of the "Lernegton" which is now for the first time made accessible to students of Talismanic Magic was done, after careful collation and edition, from numerous Ancient Manuscripts in Hebrew, Latin, and French.. New Age/Occult Pages 92

Rubaiyat Of Omar Khayyam *by Edward Fitzgerald* ISBN:*1-59462-332-5* **$13.95**
Edward Fitzgerald, whom the world has already learned, in spite of his own efforts to remain within the shadow of anonymity, to look upon as one of the rarest poets of the century, was born at Bredfield, in Suffolk, on the 31st of March, 1809. He was the third son of John Purcell... Music Pages 172

Ancient Law *by Henry Maine* ISBN: *1-59462-128-4* **$29.95**
The chief object of the following pages is to indicate some of the earliest ideas of mankind, as they are reflected in Ancient Law, and to point out the relation of those ideas to modern thought. Religion/History Pages 452

Far-Away Stories *by William J. Locke* ISBN: *1-59462-129-2* **$19.45**
"Good wine needs no bush, but a collection of mixed vintages does. And this book is just such a collection. Some of the stories I do not want to remain buried for ever in the museum files of dead magazine-numbers an author's not unpardonable vanity..." Fiction Pages 272

Life of David Crockett *by David Crockett* ISBN: *1-59462-250-7* **$27.45**
"Colonel David Crockett was one of the most remarkable men of the times in which he lived. Born in humble life, but gifted with a strong will, an indomitable courage, and unremitting perseverance.. Biographies/New Age Pages 424

Lip-Reading *by Edward Nitchie* ISBN: *1-59462-206-X* **$25.95**
Edward B. Nitchie, founder of the New York School for the Hard of Hearing, now the Nitchie School of Lip-Reading, Inc, wrote "LIP-READING Principles and Practice". The development and perfecting of this meritorious work on lip-reading was an undertaking... How-to Pages 400

A Handbook of Suggestive Therapeutics, Applied Hypnotism, Psychic Science ISBN: *1-59462-214-0* **$24.95**
by Henry Munro Health/New Age/Health/Self-help Pages 376

A Doll's House: and Two Other Plays *by Henrik Ibsen* ISBN: *1-59462-112-8* **$19.95**
Henrik Ibsen created this classic when in revolutionary 1848 Rome. Introducing some striking concepts in playwriting for the realist genre, this play has been studied the world over. Fiction/Classics/Plays 308

The Light of Asia *by sir Edwin Arnold* ISBN: *1-59462-204-3* **$13.95**
In this poetic masterpiece, Edwin Arnold describes the life and teachings of Buddha. The man who was to become known as Buddha to the world was born as Prince Gautama of India but he rejected the worldly riches and abandoned the reigns of power when... Religion/History/Biographies Pages 170

The Complete Works of Guy de Maupassant *by Guy de Maupassant* ISBN: *1-59462-157-8* **$16.95**
"For days and days, nights and nights, I had dreamed of that first kiss which was to consecrate our engagement, and I knew not on what spot I should put my lips..." Fiction/Classics Pages 240

The Art of Cross-Examination *by Francis L. Wellman* ISBN: *1-59462-309-0* **$26.95**
Written by a renowned trial lawyer, Wellman imparts his experience and uses case studies to explain how to use psychology to extract desired information through questioning. How-to/Science/Reference Pages 408

Answered or Unanswered? *by Louisa Vaughan* ISBN: *1-59462-248-5* **$10.95**
Miracles of Faith in China Religion Pages 112

The Edinburgh Lectures on Mental Science (1909) *by Thomas* ISBN: *1-59462-008-3* **$11.95**
This book contains the substance of a course of lectures recently given by the writer in the Queen Street Hall, Edinburgh. Its purpose is to indicate the Natural Principles governing the relation between Mental Action and Material Conditions... New Age/Psychology Pages 148

Ayesha *by H. Rider Haggard* ISBN: *1-59462-301-5* **$24.95**
Verily and indeed it is the unexpected that happens! Probably if there was one person upon the earth from whom the Editor of this, and of a certain previous history, did not expect to hear again... Classics Pages 380

Ayala's Angel *by Anthony Trollope* ISBN: *1-59462-352-X* **$29.95**
The two girls were both pretty; but Lucy who was twenty-one who supposed to be simple and comparatively unattractive, whereas Ayala was credited, as her Bombwhat romantic name might show, with poetic charm and a taste for romance. Ayala when her father died was nineteen... Fiction Pages 484

The American Commonwealth *by James Bryce* ISBN: *1-59462-286-8* **$34.45**
An interpretation of American democratic political theory. It examines political mechanics and society from the perspective of Scotsman James Bryce Politics Pages 572

Stories of the Pilgrims *by Margaret P. Pumphrey* ISBN: *1-59462-116-0* **$17.95**
This book explores pilgrims religious oppression in England as well as their escape to Holland and eventual crossing to America on the Mayflower, and their early days in New England... History Pages 268

QTY

The Fasting Cure *by Sinclair Upton*   ISBN: *1-59462-222-1* **$13.95**
*In the Cosmopolitan Magazine for May, 1910, and in the Contemporary Review (London) for April, 1910, I published an article dealing with my experi-
ences in fasting. I have written a great many magazine articles, but never one which attracted so much attention...* New Age/Self Help/Health Pages 164

Hebrew Astrology *by Sepharial*   ISBN: *1-59462-308-2* **$13.45**
*In these days of advanced thinking it is a matter of common observation that we have left many of the old landmarks behind and that we are now pressing
forward to greater heights and to a wider horizon than that which represented the mind-content of our progenitors...* Astrology Pages 144

Thought Vibration or The Law of Attraction in the Thought World   ISBN: *1-59462-127-6* **$12.95**
by William Walker Atkinson   Psychology/Religion Pages 144

Optimism *by Helen Keller*   ISBN: *1-59462-108-X* **$15.95**
*Helen Keller was blind, deaf, and mute since 19 months old, yet famously learned how to overcome these handicaps, communicate with the world, and
spread her lectures promoting optimism. An inspiring read for everyone...* Biographies/Inspirational Pages 84

Sara Crewe *by Frances Burnett*   ISBN: *1-59462-360-0* **$9.45**
*In the first place, Miss Minchin lived in London. Her home was a large, dull, tall one, in a large, dull square, where all the houses were alike, and all the
sparrows were alike, and where all the door-knockers made the same heavy sound...* Childrens/Classic Pages 88

The Autobiography of Benjamin Franklin *by Benjamin Franklin*   ISBN: *1-59462-135-7* **$24.95**
*The Autobiography of Benjamin Franklin has probably been more extensively read than any other American historical work, and no other book of its kind
has had such ups and downs of fortune. Franklin lived for many years in England, where he was agent...* Biographies/History Pages 332

Name	
Email	
Telephone	
Address	
City, State ZIP	

☐ **Credit Card**   ☐ **Check / Money Order**

Credit Card Number	
Expiration Date	
Signature	

Please Mail to: Book Jungle
                    PO Box 2226
                    Champaign, IL 61825
or Fax to: 630-214-0564

ORDERING INFORMATION
web: *www.bookjungle.com*
email: *sales@bookjungle.com*
fax: *630-214-0564*
mail: *Book Jungle PO Box 2226 Champaign, IL 61825*
or PayPal *to sales@bookjungle.com*

Please contact us for bulk discounts

DIRECT-ORDER TERMS

**20% Discount if You Order
Two or More Books**
Free Domestic Shipping!
Accepted: Master Card, Visa,
Discover, American Express